LITTLE NELL

LITTLE NELL

Charles Dickens

Claremont Books
London

This edition published 1995 by Claremont Books, an imprint of
Godfrey Cave Associates, 42 Bloomsbury Street, London,
WC1B 3QJ.

ISBN 1 85471 640 9

Printed and bound by Firmin-Didot (France),
Group Herissey. No d'impression : 30188.

Contents

1

The Old Curiosity Shop

She lived with her grandfather at the Old Curiosity Shop, and her name was Little Nell. He had sent her on a message one evening—she often went on messages for him, but this message had taken her a long way off from home—and on her road back she had taken a wrong turning, which is easy to do in great London, and had lost her way. And it was getting late.

She glanced timidly into the faces of the people hurrying by, and then, plucking up her courage, Little Nell accosted an old gentleman, who was not hurrying like the rest, and begged him, in a soft, sweet voice, to direct her to the street where her grandfather lived.

"It is a very long way from here, my child," said the old gentleman, stopping immediately.

"I know that, Sir," replied Nell timidly. "I am afraid it is a very long way, for I came from there tonight."

"Alone?" asked the old gentleman in some surprise.

"Oh, yes, I don't mind that, but I am a little frightened now, for I have lost my road."

"And what made you ask it of me? Suppose should tell you wrong?" said the old gentleman.

Little Nell lifted her clear eyes and looked earnestly

7

into his face. "I am sure you will not do that," she said. "You are such a very old gentleman, and walk so slow yourself."

Her answer seemed to touch the old gentleman so much that he put out his hand immediately, and said, "Come, I'll take you there."

Nell put her hand in his confidingly, and they trudged away together.

"Who has sent you so far by yourself?" asked the old gentleman.

"Somebody who is very kind to me, Sir."

"And what have you been doing?"

"That, I must not tell," said the child firmly.

The old gentleman looked at her in surprise. She might have been twelve or even thirteen years of age, but she was so small and delicately made that she looked a great deal younger. Her quick eyes seemed to read his thoughts, for she added truthfully, lifting her blue eyes frankly to his face, that there was no harm in what she had been doing, but it was a great secret—a secret which she did not even know herself.

Although her answer made him feel more curious—for it seemed strange to him that anyone should send the little girl so far from home at night—he did not question her any more, but talked cheerfully about other things till he brought her into the street that she had asked to be directed to.

Nell clapped her hands with pleasure, and, running on before, stopped at a door, remaining on the step till the old gentleman came up, and then she knocked at it.

A part of this door was glass, unprotected by any shutter, and all was very dark and silent within. By and by there was a noise as if some person were moving inside, and at length a faint light shone through the glass, and a little old man with long grey hair, worn and haggard-looking, turned the key in the lock and looked with some astonishment at such a late visitor; but Nell told him in a few words what had happened, and how her kind friend had brought her home.

"Why, bless thee, child," said the old man, patting her on the head, "how could'st thou miss thy way? What if I had lost thee, Nell!"

"I would have found my way back to *you*, Grandfather, never fear," said Nell.

The old man kissed her, then turning to the old gentleman, begged him to walk in, and closed and locked the door behind him.

Holding up the light, he led the way through a shop stocked with old and curious things. And the old man, with his haggard face so furrowed and wrinkled, seemed to match the old odd things with which the place was stored.

He led the visitor through this weird-looking place into a small sitting-room behind, in which there was another door opening into a still smaller room, where the old gentleman saw a little bed that a fairy might have slept in; it looked so very small and was so prettily arranged. The child took a candle and, tripping into this room, left her grandfather and the old gentleman together.

"You must be tired, Sir," said the first, as he placed a chair near the fire. "How can I thank you?"

"By taking more care of your grandchild another time, my good friend," said the old gentleman.

"More care!" cried the old man in a shrill voice; "more care of Nelly! Why, who ever loved a child as I love Nell?"

"I don't think you consider—" the visitor began.

"I don't consider!" cried the old man, interrupting him. "I don't consider her! Ah, you little know of the truth! Little Nelly, Little Nelly!"

It would be impossible for any man to express more affection than the old man did in these four words. He said nothing more, but, resting his chin upon his hand, and shaking his head twice or thrice, fixed his eyes on the fire.

While they were sitting thus in silence the door of the tiny room opened, and Nell returned, and busied herself in preparing supper. She appeared to be his little housekeeper, for there was no one else about the place. And the old man motioned the visitor to approach the table.

They had hardly begun their repast when there was a knock at the shop door, and Nell, bursting into a hearty laugh, said it was dear old Kit at last.

"Foolish Nell," said the old man, fondling her hair; "she always laughs at poor Kit."

Nell laughed again, and her new friend smiled in sympathy, glad to think she could laugh so merrily in that strange, weird, dismal place.

The old man took up a candle and went to open the door, and brought back Kit with him.

Kit was a shockheaded, shambling, awkward lad with an uncommonly wide mouth, very red cheeks, a turned-up nose, and a most comical expression of face. He was the errand-boy of the Old Curiosity Shop.

"A long way, wasn't it, Kit?" said the little old man.

"Why, then, it was a goodish stretch, Master."

Kit had a remarkable manner of standing sideways as he spoke, and thrusting his head forwards over his shoulder. Nell was so tickled at him that she laughed again, and Kit, quite flattered at her doing so, tried to look grave, but, not succeeding in his efforts, burst into a loud roar and laughed violently; then, carrying a large slice of bread and meat and a mug of beer into a corner, he set upon his supper directly.

The old man took no notice of what passed, but stared fixedly at the fire; and then, turning to the visitor, said, with a sigh, "You don't know what you say when you tell me I don't consider her. Come hither, Nell."

The little girl hastened from her seat, and put her arm about his neck.

"Do I love thee, Nell?" said he. "Say, do I love thee, Nell, or no?"

"Indeed, indeed you do," replied the child with great earnestness. "Kit knows you do."

"Nobody is such a fool as to say he doesn't," bawled Kit, putting a monstrous piece of bread and meat into his mouth.

"She is poor now" said the old man, patting the child's cheek, "but the time is coming when she shall be rich."

"I am very happy as I am, Grandfather," said Nell.

"Tush, tush!" returned the old man, "thou dost not know—how should'st thou?" Then he muttered again between his teeth, and, sighing, looked into the fire, forgetful of everything around him.

By this time it was nearly midnight, and Nell's kind friend rose to go.

"One moment, Sir," said the old man rousing up. "Now, Kit, near midnight, boy, and you still here! Get home, get home, and be true to your time in the morning, for there's work to do. Good night. There, bid him good night, Nell, and let him begone."

"Good night, Kit," said Nell, her eyes lighting up with merriment and kindness.

"And thank this gentleman," interposed his master,

"but for whose care I might have lost my little girl tonight."

"No, no, Master," said Kit, "that won't do, that won't!"

"What do you mean?" cried the old man.

"I'd have found her, Master," said Kit. "I'd have found her. I'd bet that I'd find her if she was above ground, I would, as quick as anybody, Master. Ha, ha, ha!" And Kit, gradually backing to the door, roared himself out.

"I haven't seemed to thank you, Sir, enough for what you have done tonight," said the grandfather, turning to the old gentleman, while Nell cleared the table; "but I do thank you humbly and heartily, and so does she, and her thanks are better worth than mine. I should be sorry that you went away and thought I was unmindful of your goodness, or careless of her—I am not, indeed."

"I am sure of that," returned the old gentleman, "from what I have seen. But," he added, "may I ask you a question?"

"Ay, Sir," replied the grandfather. "What is it?"

"This delicate child," said the old gentleman, "with so much beauty and intelligence—has she nobody to care for her but you? Has she no other companion or adviser?"

"No," said the grandfather, looking anxiously into his face. "No, and she wants no other. Waking or sleeping, by night or day, in sickness or health, she is the one object of my care, and if you knew of how much care, you would look on me with different eyes, you would indeed. Ah! it's a weary life for an old man—a weary, weary life; but there is a great end to gain, and that I keep before me."

The old gentleman, seeing that the grandfather was getting excited and impatient, said nothing more, but turned to put on an outer coat which he had thrown off on entering the room, and was surprised to see the child standing patiently by with a cloak upon her arm, and in her hand a hat and stick.

"Those are not mine, my dear," said he.

"No," returned the child quietly, "they are grandfather's."

"But he is not going out tonight?"

"Oh, yes he is," said Nell, with a smile.

"And what becomes of you, my pretty one?"

"Me! I stay here, of course. I always do."

The old gentleman looked in astonishment towards the grandfather, who pretended to be busy with his cloak. Then he looked back to the slight, gentle figure of the little girl. Alone! In that gloomy place all the long, dreary night!

Nell took no notice of his surprise, but helped her grandfather with his cloak, and when he was ready she took a candle to light them to the door.

The old gentleman, in his anxiety for the child, hesitated; but the grandfather signed to him to pass out of the room first, and he could do nothing but comply.

When they reached the door, Nell put down her candle and raised her face to kiss the old gentleman who had brought her home. Then she ran to her grandfather, who folded her in his arms, and bade God bless her.

"Sleep soundly, Nell," he said in a low voice, "and angels guard thy bed! Do not forget thy prayers, my sweet. Early in the morning I shall be home."

"You'll not ring twice," said Nell. "The bell wakes me even in the middle of a dream." Then she opened the door, and held it until both of them had passed out.

Her grandfather paused a moment while it was closed and fastened on the inside, and, satisfied that all was

secure, walked on at a slow pace. At the corner of the
street he stopped, and, looking with a troubled face at
Nell's kind friend, said that their ways were widely
different, and that he must take his leave; and hurried
away before the old gentleman could stop him, looking
over his shoulder suspiciously to be certain he was not
being followed.

The old gentleman stood where he had left him,
wondering what this mystery was, unwilling to go away.

What made that old man leave that small, slight girl
alone in that dismal place? And where was he going
himself so late at night? He went back to the house and
stopped and listened at the door, but it was dark now, and
silent as the grave.

"Stay here, of course," the child had said in answer to
his question, "I always do!"

What *could* take that strange old man from home by
night, and every night? And thinking of his haggard face,
his restless, wandering looks, he grew more anxious
still; and lingered about, and could not tear himself
away, thinking of all possible harm that might happen to
the child.

The clocks struck one. Still he was pacing the street.
Then it began to rain—rain heavily; and the old
gentleman, tired out, engaged the nearest coach and
drove away.

2

An Unwelcome Relation

A week later the old man and a young one seemed to be having a quarrel at the Old Curiosity Shop, for their voices were loud and high.

"If oaths, or prayers, or words could rid me of you," the old man cried, "they should! I would be quit of you, and would be relieved if you were dead."

"I know it," retorted the other. "But neither oaths, nor prayers, nor words, will kill me, and therefore I live, and mean to live."

"And his mother died!" cried the old man, passionately clasping his hands and looking upwards; "and this is Heaven's justice!"

The other stood lounging with his foot upon a chair and regarded the old man with a contemptuous sneer. He was a young man of one-and-twenty, or thereabouts; well made, and certainly handsome, but with a dissipated and insolent air which only repelled one.

"Justice or no justice," said the young fellow, "here I am, and here I shall stop till such time as I think fit to go, unless you send for assistance to put me out—which you won't do, I know. I tell you again that I want to see my sister."

"*Your sister*," said the old man bitterly.

'Ah! You can't change the relationship," said the young fellow. "If you could, you'd have done it long ago. I want to see my sister that you keep cooped up here, poisoning her mind with your sly secrets, and pretending an affection for her that you may work her to death, and add a few scraped shillings every week to the money you can hardly count. I want to see her; and I will!"

"Why do you hunt and persecute me, God help me?" cried the old man, turning on his grandson. "How often am I to tell you that my life is one of care and self-denial, and that I am poor?"

"How often am I to tell you," retorted the other, looking coldly at him, "that I know better?"

"You have chosen your own path," said the old man; "leave Nell and me to toil and work."

"Nell will be a woman soon," returned the other, "and, bred in your faith, she'll forget her brother unless he shows himself sometimes."

"Take care," said the old man, with sparkling eyes, "that she does not forget you when you would have her memory keenest. Take care that the day doesn't come when you walk barefoot in the streets, and she rides in a gay carriage of her own."

"You mean when she has your money?" retorted the young man. "How like a poor man he talks!"

"And yet," said the old man, dropping his voice and speaking like one who thinks aloud, "how poor we are, and what a life it is! The cause is a young child's, guiltless of all harm or wrong, but nothing goes well with it! Hope and patience, hope and patience! "

The words were uttered in too low a tone to reach the young man's ears. Suddenly the door opened and Nell herself appeared. She was closely followed by an elderly man, so low in stature as to be quite a dwarf, though his head and face were large enough for the body of a giant. He had a dirty, unwholesome face, with black, sly, cunning eyes, and he wore a ghastly smile. Such hair as he had was of a grizzled black, cut short and straight on his temples, and hanging in a frowsy fringe about his ears. His hands were very dirty; and his finger-nails were crooked, long, and yellow.

Nell advanced timidly towards her brother and put her hand in his, and the old curiosity dealer, who had not expected his uncouth visitor, seemed somewhat embarrassed.

"Ah!" said the dwarf, surveying the young man attentively, "that should be your grandson, neighbour."

"Say rather that he should not be," replied the old man. "But he is."

"Well, Nelly," said the young fellow, "do they teach you to hate me, eh?"

"No, no! For shame! Oh, no!" cried Nell.

"To love me, perhaps?" said her brother with a sneer.

"But I do indeed love you, and always will," repeated Nell with great emotion; "but oh! if you would leave off vexing him and making him unhappy, then I could love you more."

"I see!" said the young man, as he stooped carelessly over the child, and, having kissed her, pushed her from him. "There—get you away now you have said your lesson. You needn't whimper. We part good friends enough, if that's the matter."

He followed her with his eyes until she had gained her little room and closed the door; and then, turning to the dwarf, said abruptly, "Harkee, Mr—"

"Meaning me?" returned the dwarf. "Quilp is my

name. You might remember. It's not a long one— Daniel
Quilp."

"Harkee, Mr Quilp, then. You have some influence
with my grandfather there?"

"Some," said Mr Quilp.

"And are in a few of his mysteries and secrets?"

"A few," replied Quilp with equal dryness.

"Then let me tell him once for all, through you, that I
will come into and go out of this place as often as I like,
so long as he keeps Nell here. I *will* see her when I
please. That's my point. I came here today to maintain it,
and I'll come here fifty times with the same object and
always with the same success. I said I would stop till I
had gained it. I have done so, and now my visit is
ended." With that he flung himself out of the shop.

"Humph!" said the dwarf, "so much for dear relations!
Thank God, I acknowledge none! Nor need you either,"
he added, turning to the old man, "if you were not as
weak as a reed, and nearly as senseless."

"What would you have me do?" retorted the old man
in a kind of helpless desperation. "It is easy to talk and
sneer. What would you have me do?"

"What would I do if *I* was in your case?" said the
dwarf.

"Something violent, no doubt."

"You're right there," returned the dwarf, grinning like
a fiend as he rubbed his dirty hands together, and
appearing quite horrible with his monstrous head and
little body.

"Here," he said, putting his hand into his breast and
sidling up to the old man as he spoke; "I brought it for
fear of accidents, as, being in gold, it was something
large and heavy for Nell to carry in her bag. Neighbour, I
would I knew in what good investment all these supplies

are sunk. But you are a deep man, and keep your secret close."

"My secret!" said the other with a haggard look. "Yes, you're right—I—I keep it close—very close."

He said no more, but, taking the money which the dwarf had brought with him, turned away with a slow, uncertain step, and pressed his hand upon his head like a weary, dejected man. The dwarf watched him sharply, while he passed into the little sitting-room, and locked it in an iron safe above the chimney-piece.

And after musing for a short space, Mr Quilp prepared to take his leave.

When he was gone Nell brought some needlework to the table, and sat by the old man's side. It was pleasant to see fresh flowers in the room, her pet bird with a green bough shading his little cage. It was curious to turn from the beauty and grace of the girl, to the stooping figure, careworn face, and jaded aspect of the old man. As he grew weaker and more feeble, what would become of this lonely little creature? He had always had a large and affectionate heart, and those upon whom he had lavished its best love were gone—all gone; all but this one frail child.

First of all there had been his little brother, a sickly child, for whom the elder brother denied himself the sports he loved to sit beside his couch, or to carry him in his arms to some green spot.

The sickly boy, shielded by his care, grew to manhood, grew well and strong. And then there came a time when both brothers fixed their love upon the same beautiful girl.

The younger brother's heart was full of those old days. He left his brother to be happy, and went abroad. The elder brother married the beautiful girl, who soon died, and left a little daughter behind.

Nell was the child of this daughter, the old man's darling daughter, whom he had loved so well, and who had made a wretched marriage, and had also died, leaving to her father's care two children—one a boy of twelve, the other a girl, an infant child—little Nell.

The old man, grandfather to these two orphans, was now a broken man, crushed, not so much by age, as by the heavy hand of sorrow.

With the loss of his fortune (for his daughter's husband had ruined him) he began to trade—in pictures first—and then in ancient, curious things, and opened the Old Curiosity Shop.

The boy grew like his spendthrift father in mind and person, and soon spurned the shelter of the old man's roof to live with those as wild and wasteful as himself. The girl so like her mother, that when the old man had her on his knee, and looked into her sweet, blue eyes, he felt as if his daughter were a little child again.

Fred's wild ways drained him of his money, and a fear began to trouble him that Nell should come to poverty and want. It haunted him night and day. It was then he took to borrowing money of the dwarf, and leaving the house at night to trade with it in that mysterious, secret way, which nobody yet had guessed—the secret way by which he fondly hoped to win a fortune for Nell.

"When I think," he said, putting his hand upon the child's head, as she sat sewing by his side, "of the many years—many in thy short life—that thou hast lived alone with me, and in which thou hast lived apart from nearly all thy kind but one old man, I sometimes fear that I have dealt hardly by thee, Nell."

"Grandfather!" cried Nell, looking up in surprise.

"Not in intention—not so," said he. "But if I should be forced to leave thee, meanwhile, how have I fitted thee for struggles with the world? Hark! I hear Kit outside. Go to him, Nell."

She rose, and hurrying away, stopped, turned back, and put her arms about the old man's neck, then hurried away again.

Kit had come for a writing lesson which Nell gave him twice a week. The lesson was given. The evening passed, and night came on. The old man quitted the house secretly at the same hour as before; and the child was once more left alone within its gloomy walls.

3

Nell's Visit to the Dwarf

Mr Quilp had just finished his breakfast, and was now on his way to the riverside, where he took a boat for the wharf, situated on the opposite shore, where he carried on his business.

He was put ashore hard by the wharf, and proceeded thither through a narrow lane, dirty with river-water and mud. Arrived at his destination, the first object that presented itself to his view was a boy standing on his head, who was speedily brought on his heels by the sound of his master's voice; and as soon as his head was in its right position, Mr Quilp punched it immediately.

"Come, you let me alone," said the boy, parrying the blows; "you'll get something you won't like if you don't, and so I tell you."

"You dog!" snarled the dwarf. "I'll beat you with an iron rod, I'll scratch you with a rusty nail, I'll pinch your eyes, if you talk to me, I will!"

With these threats he clenched his hand again, and catching the boy's head as it dodged from side to side, gave it three or four good hard knocks.

"You won't do it again," said the boy, nodding his head and drawing back, "now—"

"Stand still, you dog," said Quilp. "I won't do it again, because I've done it as often as I want. Here. Take the key."

"Why don't you hit one of your size?" said the boy approaching very slowly.

"Where is there one of my size, you dog?" returned the dwarf. "Take the key, or I'll brain you with it. Now open the counting-house."

The boy sulkily complied. There existed a strange kind of mutual liking between this boy and the dwarf Quilp would certainly suffer nobody to contradict him but the boy, and the boy would not have submitted himself to be knocked about by anybody but Quilp, when he had the power to run away at any time he chose.

"Now," said Quilp, passing into the wooden counting-house, "you mind the wharf. Stand upon your head again, and I'll cut one of your feet off."

It was a dirty little box, the counting-house, with nothing in it but a rickety desk and two stools. Quilp pulled his hat over his brows, climbed on the desk (which had a flat top), and, stretching his short length upon it, went to sleep, to make up for a bad night.

He had not been asleep a quarter of an hour when the boy opened the door and thrust in his head, which was like a bundle of badly-picked oakum. Quilp was a light sleeper, and started up directly.

"Here's somebody for you," said the boy.

"Who?"

"I don't know."

"Ask!" said Quilp, seizing a large piece of jagged wood and throwing it at him with such dexterity that it was well the boy disappeared before it reached the spot on which he had stood. "Ask, you dog!"

The boy not caring to appear again, discreetly sent the visitor in his stead, who now appeared in the doorway.

"What, Nelly!" cried Quilp.

"Yes—" said the child, hesitating whether to enter or retreat, for the dwarf, just roused, with his dishevelled hair hanging all about him, and a yellow handkerchief over his head, was something fearful to behold, "It's only me, Sir."

"Come in," said Quilp, without getting off the desk. "What is your message, Nelly?"

She handed him a letter; and Quilp proceeded to read it. He was evidently perplexed by the contents of the letter; he opened his eyes very wide, and frowned horribly, scratched his head, and ended with a long whistle of surprise and dismay.

"Halloa, here!" he said at last, in a voice which made the child start as though a gun had been fired off at her ear, "Nelly! "

"Yes, Sir?"

"Do you know what's inside this letter, Nell?"

"No, Sir."

"Are you sure, quite sure, quite certain, upon your soul?"

"Quite sure, Sir."

"Well," muttered Quilp, as he marked her earnest look, "I believe you. Hump! Gone already? Gone in four-and-twenty hours! What has he done with it now? That's the mystery!"

He bit his nails, and scratched his head again. Then added, "You look very pretty today, Nelly, charmingly pretty. Are you tired, Nelly?"

"No, Sir. I'm in a hurry to get back, for he will be anxious while I am away."

"There's no hurry, little Nell, no hurry at all. You shall come with me to Tower Hill and see Mrs Quilp," said the dwarf. "She's very fond of you, Nell, though not so fond as I am. You shall come home with me."

"I must go back indeed," said Nell. "Grandfather told me to return directly I had the answer."

"But you haven't had it, Nelly," retorted the dwarf, "and won't have it, and can't have it, until I have been home; so you see that to do your errand you must go with me. Reach me yonder my hat, my dear, and we'll go directly."

Quilp led the way from the counting-house to the wharf outside, when the first objects that presented themselves were the boy who had stood on his head, and another lad of his own size, rolling in the mud together, and cuffing each other with mutual heartiness.

"It's Kit!" cried Nelly, clasping her hands; "poor Kit who came with me! Oh, pray stop them, Mr Quilp."

"I'll stop 'em." And Quilp, diving into the counting-house, returned with a thick stick. "I'll stop 'em. Now, my boys, fight away. I'll fight you both. I'll take both of you, both together, both together!"

The dwarf flourished his cudgel and, dancing round the combatants, trod upon them and skipped over them in a kind of frenzy, laying about him in a most desperate manner, and dealing such blows that none but the veriest little savage would have inflicted.

The boys soon scrambled to their feet and called for quarter.

"I'll beat you to a pulp, you dogs!" cried Quilp, trying to get at either of them for a parting blow; "I'll bruise your faces till you're copper-coloured, I will!"

"Come, you drop that stick, or it'll be the worse for you," said the boy, dodging round him, and watching for an opportunity to rush in: "you drop that stick."

"Come a little nearer, and I'll drop it on your skull, you dog; a little nearer—nearer yet."

But the boy declined the invitation until his master

was a little off his guard, when he darted in and, seizing
the weapon, tried to wrest it from his grasp. Quilp, who
was as strong as a lion, easily kept his hold until the boy
was tugging at it with his utmost power, when he
suddenly let it go and sent him reeling backwards, so
that the boy fell violently upon his head.

This tickled the dwarf so much that he laughed and
stamped with delight.

"Never mind," said the boy, nodding his head and
rubbing it at the same time; "you see if ever I offer to
strike anybody again because they say you're an uglier
dwarf than can be seen anywhere for a penny, that's all."

"Do you mean to say I'm not, you dog?" said Quilp.

"No!" retorted the boy.

"Then what do you fight for on my wharf, you
villain?"

"Because he said so," replied the boy, pointing at Kit,
"not because you ain't."

"Then why did he say," bawled Kit, "that Miss Nelly
was ugly, and that she and my master was obliged to do
whatever his master liked? Why did he say that?"

"He said what he did because he's a fool, and you said
what you did because you're very wise and clever.
Always speak the truth, Kit. At all times speak the truth.
Lock the counting-house, you dog, and bring me the
key."

The other boy did as he was told, and was rewarded for
taking his master's part by a dexterous rap on the nose
with a key, which brought the water into his eyes.

Then Mr Quilp departed with Nelly and Kit in a boat,
and the boy revenged himself by dancing on his head at
intervals on the extreme edge of the wharf, during the
whole time they crossed the river.

"Here's Nelly Trent, dear Mrs Quilp," said her

husband, taking Nell into the house with him while Kit waited outside. "A glass of wine, my dear, and a biscuit, for she has had a long walk. She'll sit with you, my soul, while I write a letter."

Mrs Quilp, a pretty, timid little woman, looked trembling into her husband's face to know why he spoke in such a kindly manner—it not being his usual way—and obedient to his summons, for he had beckoned her to go out with him, she followed him into the next room.

"Mind what I say to you," whispered Quilp. "See if you can get out of her anything about her grandfather, or what they do, or how they live, or what he tells her. I've my reasons for knowing. And you have a soft mild way with you that'll win upon her. Do you hear?"

"Yes, Quilp."

"Go then. What's the matter now?"

"Dear Quilp," faltered his wife, "I love the child—if you *could* do without making me deceive her—"

The dwarf muttered a terrible oath, and looked round as if for some weapon to strike her with. The submissive little woman hurriedly entreated him not to be angry, and promised to do as he bade her.

"Do you hear me?" whispered Quilp, nipping and pinching her arm; "worm yourself into her secrets; I know you can. I'm listening, recollect. If you're not sharp enough I'll creak the door, and woe betide you if I have to creak it much. Go!"

Mrs Quilp departed according to order, and her amiable husband, hiding himself behind the partly opened door, put his ear close to it, and began to listen with a face of great craftiness and attention.

Poor Mrs Quilp was thinking in what manner to begin, and it was not until the door, creaking in a very urgent manner, warned her to proceed.

"How very often you have come backwards and forwards lately to Mr Quilp, my dear."

"I have said so to grandfather a hundred times," returned Nell innocently.

"And what has he said to that?"

"Only sighed, and dropped his head, and seemed so sad and wretched that if you could have seen him I am sure you must have cried. How that door creaks!"

"It often does," returned Mrs Quilp, with an uneasy glance towards it. "But your grandfather—he used not to be so wretched?"

"Oh, no!" said the child eagerly, "so different! We were once so happy, and he so cheerful and contented! You cannot think what a sad change has fallen on us since."

"I am very very sorry to hear you speak like this, my dear!" said Mrs Quilp. And she spoke the truth.

"Thank you," returned Nell, kissing her cheek, "you are always kind to me, and it is a pleasure to talk to you. I can speak to no one else about him, but poor Kit. You cannot think how it grieves me to see him alter so."

"He'll alter again, Nelly, and be what he was before."

"Oh, if God would only let that come about!" said Nell, with tears in her eyes; "but it is a long time now since he first began to—I thought I saw that door moving."

"It's the wind," began Mrs Quilp faintly. "Began to—?"

"To be so thoughtful and dejected," said the child. "I used to read to him by the fireside, and he sat listening, and when I stopped and we began to talk, he told me about my mother, and how she once looked and spoke just like me when she was a little child. We were very happy once!"

"Nelly, Nelly!" said the poor woman, "I can't bear to see one as young as you so sorrowful. Pray don't cry."

"I do so very seldom," said Nell, "but I have kept this to myself a long time, and I am not quite well, I think, for the tears come into my eyes and I cannot keep them back. I don't mind telling you my grief, for I know you will not tell it to anyone again."

Mrs Quilp turned away her head and made no answer.

"Then," said the child, "we often walked in the fields and among green trees. But now we never have these walks, and though it is the same house it is darker and much more gloomy than it used to be."

She paused here; but though the door creaked more than once Mrs Quilp said nothing.

"Mind you don't suppose," said Nell earnestly, "that grandfather is less kind to me than he was. I think he loves me better every day, and is kinder and more affectionate than he was the day before. You do not know how fond he is of me!"

"I am sure he loves you dearly," said Mrs Quilp.

"Indeed, indeed he does!" cried Nell, "as dearly as I love him. But I have not told you the greatest change of all, and this you must not breathe again to any one. He has no sleep or rest, but that which he takes by day in his easy chair; for every night, and nearly all night long, he is away from home."

"Nelly!"

"Hush!" said the child, laying her finger on her lip and looking round. "When he comes home in the morning, which is generally just before day, I let him in. Last night he was very late, and it was quite light. I saw that his face was deadly pale, and that his eyes were bloodshot, and that his legs trembled as he walked. When I had gone to bed again, I heard him groan. I got up and ran back to him, and heard him say, before he knew I was there, that he could not bear his life much longer, and that if it was not for the child he would wish to die. What shall I do? Oh I what shall I do?"

The fountains of her heart were opened; the child, overpowered by the weight of her sorrows, by the first confidence she had ever shown, and by the sympathy with which her tale had been received, hid her face in the arms of her helpless friend, and burst into a passion of tears.

In a few moments Mr Quilp returned and looked quite surprised to find that Nell had been crying. "She's tired, you see, Mrs Quilp," said the dwarf, squinting horribly. "It's a long way from her home to the wharf, and then she was alarmed to see a couple of young scoundrels fighting, and was timorous on the water besides. All this together has been too much for her. Poor Nell!"

Quilp patted her on her head; but Nell shrank so quickly from his touch, and was so anxious to get out of his reach, that she rose directly, and said she was ready to go.

"Well, if you will go, you wi!l, Nelly. Here's the note. It's only to say that I shall see him tomorrow or maybe the next day, and that I couldn't do that little business for him this morning. Goodbye, Nelly. Here you, sir, take care of her, d'ye hear?"

Kit, who appeared at the summons, did not deign to make any reply to so unnecessary a charge, and followed his young mistress, who had by this time taken her leave of Mrs Quilp.

"You're a keen questioner, an't you, Mrs Quilp?" said the dwarf, turning upon her as soon as they were left alone.

"I am very sorry for the child, Quilp," said his wife.

"Surely I have done enough. I have led her on to tell her secret when she supposed we were alone, and you were by, God forgive me!"

"You led her on! You did a great deal, truly! What did I tell you about making me creak the door? It's lucky for you that from what she let fall, I've got the clue I want, for if I hadn't, I'd have visited the failure upon you. But you may thank your fortunate stars that I'm on the old gentleman's track, and have got a new light. So let me hear no more about this matter now, or at any other time; and don't get anything too nice for dinner, for I shan't be home to it."

4

The Old Man's Secret

Nelly, in her confidence with Mrs Quilp, had not described half of the sadness and sorrow of her thoughts, or the heaviness of the cloud which overhung her home.

It was not the sad days she passed; not the dark, dreary evenings, nor the long, solitary nights, that had wrung the tears from Nell. It was to see the old man, whom she loved so well, and who returned her love so dearly, struck down beneath the pressure of some hidden grief. She had a dreadful fear, sometimes, that his mind was wandering; for he spoke strangely, often, and was so restless and unhappy since he had taken to spending the long, long nights away, that she had a terrible fear that in one of his despondent fits he might take his life, perhaps.

They were alone in the world—she and her aged grandfather; and there was no one to help, or advise, or care about them, she knew.

He talked so wildly of her being rich some day, though they lived so poorly now; and his anxiety for riches had only come about since he had begun to spend the nights from home.

One night, the third night after Nelly's interview with Mrs Quilp, the old man, who had been weak and ill all day, said he should not leave home. Nell's eyes sparkled at the news, but she looked anxiously at his worn and sickly face.

"Two days," he said, "two whole, clear days have passed, and there is no reply. What *did* he tell thee, Nell?"

"Exactly what I told you, Grandfather, indeed."

"True," said the old man faintly. "Yes. But tell me again, Nell. My head fails me. What was it that he told thee? Nothing more than that he would see me tomorrow or next day? That was in the note."

"Nothing more," said the child. "Shall I go to him again tomorrow, dear Grandfather? Very early? I will be there and back before breakfast."

The old man shook his head, and, sighing mournfully, drew her towards him. "'Twould be no use, my dear, no earthly use. But if he deserts me, Nell, at this moment— if he deserts me now, I am ruined. If we were beggars!"

"What if we are?" said Nell boldly. "Let us be beggars, and be happy."

"Beggars—and happy!" said the old man. "Poor child!"

"Dear Grandfather," cried Nell, with an energy which shone in her flushed face and trembling voice. "I am not a child in that, I think; but even if I am, oh! hear me, pray, that we may beg, or work in open roads or fields to earn a scanty living, rather than live as we do now."

"Nelly!" exclaimed the old man.

"Yes, yes, rather than live as we do now," Nell repeated, more earnestly than before. "If you are sorrowful let me know why, and let me be sorrowful too; if you waste away and are paler every day, let me try to comfort you. If you are poor, let us be poor together; but let me be with you; do not let me see such change and not know why, or I shall break my heart, and die. Dear

Grandfather, let us leave this place tomorrow, and beg our way from door to door."

The old man covered his face with his hands, and hid it in the pillow of the couch on which he lay.

"Let us be beggars," said the child, passing an arm round his neck; "I have no fear but that we shall have enough; I am sure we shall. Let us walk through country places, and sleep in fields and under trees, and never think of money again, or of anything that can make you sad; but rest at nights, and have the sun and wind upon our faces in the day, and thank God together. And when you are tired, you shall stop to rest in the pleasantest place that we can find, and I will go and beg for both."

The child's voice was lost in sobs as she dropped upon the old man's shoulder; and they wept together.

Neither of them saw that the dwarf had glided in, greedily listening to all that Nell had said. They were so earnest in their grief that neither had heard him enter. Quilp, noting this, skipped with uncommon agility upon a chair, perching himself on the back with his feet on the seat; and with his head turned on one side, and his ugly features twisted into a complacent grin, he sat listening and watching craftily.

The child uttered a shriek when she lifted her head and saw the dwarf; and the old man, half doubting his reality, looked shrinkingly at him.

Not at all disconcerted, Quilp merely nodded with great condescension; and the old man, pronouncing his name at last, inquired how he came there.

"Through the door," said Quilp, pointing over his shoulder with his thumb. "I'm not quite small enough to get through keyholes. I wish I was. I want to have some talk with you particularly, and in private—with nobody present, neighbour. Goodbye, little Nelly."

Nell looked at the old man, who nodded to her to retire, and kissed her cheek.

"Once, and once for all," he said, lifting his bowed head when she was gone, "have you brought me any money?"

"No!" returned Quilp.

"Then," said the old man, clenching his hands desperately, and looking upward, "the child and I are lost!"

"Neighbour," said Quilp sternly, "you have no secret from me now."

The old man looked up, trembling.

"You are surprised," said Quilp. "Well, perhaps that's natural. You have no secrets from me now, I say; no, not one. For now I know that all those sums of money, that all those loans that you have had from me, have found their way to—shall I say the word?"

"Ay," replied the old man, "say it, if you will."

"To the gaming table," rejoined the dwarf, "your nightly haunt. This was the precious scheme to make your fortune, was it?"

The secret was out at last. The long nights he had spent from home had been passed in gambling—playing cards for money—by which the old man fondly hoped to make a fortune. Not only had he wasted his own hard-earned savings in this way, but all the large sums he had borrowed at heavy interest from the dwarf. They were gone! All gone!

"Yes," cried the old man, turning upon him with gleaming eyes, "it was. It is. It will be till I die!"

"That I should have been blinded," said Quilp, looking contemptuously at him, "by a mere shallow gambler!"

"I am not a gambler," cried the old man fiercely. "I call to Heaven that every piece I staked, I whispered to myself that orphan's name, and called on Heaven to bless the venture."

"When did you first begin this mad career?" asked Quilp, subdued by the old man's grief and wildness.

"When did I first begin?" He passed his hand across his brow. "When was it that I first began? When should it be, but when I first began to think how little I had saved; and how she would be left to the rough mercies of the world; then it was that I began to think about it."

"You lost what money you had laid by first, and then you came to me. While I thought you were making your fortune (as you said you were) you were making yourself a beggar, eh? Dear me! And so it comes to pass that I hold every security you could scrape together, and a bill-of-sale upon the—upon the stock and property," Quilp said, standing up and looking about him, as if to assure himself that none of it had been taken away. "But did you never win?"

"Never!" groaned the old man. "Never won back my loss!"

"I thought," sneered the dwarf, "that if a man played long enough he was sure to win at last, or at the worst not to come off a loser."

"And so he is," cried the old man, suddenly rousing himself from his state of despondency, and lashed into the most violent excitement, "so he is; I have felt that from the first; I have always known it; I've seen it; I never felt it half so strongly as I feel it now. Quilp, I have dreamed three nights of winning the same large sum; I could never dream that dream before, though I have often tried. Do not desert me now that I have this chance. I have no resource but you; give me some help; let me try this one last hope."

The dwarf shrugged his shoulders and shook his head.

"I only want a little help once more; a few pounds, but two score pounds, dear Quilp."

"The last was seventy," said the dwarf, "and it went in one night."

"I know it did. Quilp, consider, consider, that orphan child! If I were alone, I could die with gladness. Help me for her sake, I implore you—not for mine; for hers!"

"I am sorry I have an appointment in the City," said Quilp; and he rose to go.

"Nay, Quilp, good Quilp," gasped the old man, catching at his coat; "do not be hard upon me. You are a great gainer by me. Oh! spare me the money for this one last hope!"

"I couldn't really," said Quilp, with unusual politeness; "I was so deceived by the humble way in which you lived alone with Nelly, your miserly way, and the reputation you had among those who knew of your being rich, that I'd have advanced money to you even now, on your simple note of hand, if I had not unexpectedly learned your secret way of life."

"Who is it?" cried the old man desperately, "that, notwithstanding all my caution, told you that? Come. Let me know the name—the person."

"Now, who do you think?" said the crafty dwarf.

"It was Kit; it must have been the boy; he played the spy, and you tampered with him."

"How came you to think of him?" returned the dwarf. "Yes, it was Kit. Poor Kit!"

So saying, he nodded in a friendly manner, and took his leave, stopping when he had passed the outer door a little distance, and grinning with extraordinary delight.

"Poor Kit!" muttered Quilp. "I think it was Kit who said I was an uglier dwarf than could be seen anywhere for a penny; wasn't it? Ha, ha, ha! Poor Kit!"

And with that he went his way, still chuckling as he went.

5

The Old Man's Illness

Kit sat eating his supper in his mother's little room—a very poor and homely place, but spotlessly clean and neat—while she was still hard at work at an ironing-table.

"Old master an't gone out tonight," said Kit.

And his mother rejoined, "It's a cruel thing to keep the dear child shut up there."

"He don't think it's cruel, bless you," said Kit, "and don't mean to be so, or he wouldn't do it; I do consider, Mother, that he wouldn't do it for all the gold and silver in the world. No, no, that he wouldn't. I know him better nor that."

"Then what does he do it for, and why does he keep it so close from you?" said Mrs Nubbles.

"That I don't know," said Kit. "If he hadn't tried to keep it so close, though, I should never have found it out; for it was his getting me away at night, and sending me off so much earlier than he used to, that first made me curious to know what was going on. Hark! what's that?"

"It's only somebody outside."

"It's somebody crossing over here," said Kit, standing up to listen, "and coming very fast, too."

The footsteps drew nearer, the door was opened with a hasty hand, and Nell herself, pale and breathless, and hastily wrapped in a few disordered garments, hurried into the room.

"Miss Nelly! What is the matter?" cried mother and son together.

"I must not stay a moment," she returned; "Grandfather has been taken very ill; I found him in a fit upon the floor—"

"I'll run for a doctor" said Kit, seizing his hat; "I'll be there directly, I'll—"

"No, no," cried Nell, "there is one there, and you're not wanted; you—you must never come near us any more!"

"What!" roared Kit.

"Never again," said Nell. "Don't ask me why, for I don't know. Pray don't ask me why, pray don't be sorry, pray don't be vexed with me! I have nothing to do with it, indeed!"

Kit looked at her with his eyes stretched wide, and opened and shut his mouth a great many times, but couldn't get out one word.

"He complains and raves of you," said Nell. "I don't know what you have done, but I hope it's nothing very bad."

"*I* done!" roared Kit.

"He cries that you are the cause of all his misery," returned Nell with tears in her eyes; "he screamed and called for you. They say you must not come near him or he will die. You must not return to us any more. I came to tell you. I thought it would be better that I should come than somebody quite strange. O Kit, what have you done? You, in whom I trusted so much, and who were almost the only friend I had!"

The unfortunate Kit looked at his young mistress harder and harder, and with eyes growing wider and wider, but could not speak.

"I have brought his money for the week," said Nell, looking at Mrs Nubbles, and laying it on the table, "and—and—a little more, for he was always good and kind to me. I hope he will be sorry and do well somewhere else, and not take this to heart too much. It grieves me very much to part from him like this, but there is no help. It must be done. Good night!"

With the tears streaming down her face, and her slight figure trembling with agitation, and a thousand painful and affectionate feelings, Nelly hastened to the door, and disappeared as rapidly as she had come.

Mrs Nubbles rocked herself upon a chair, wringing her hands and weeping bitterly; but Kit made no attempt to comfort her, and remained quite bewildered.

Next morning the old man was in a raging fever, accompanied with delirium, and in peril of his life. The old house was no longer solitary, for, besides the hired nurses who had come to tend him, Quilp was in possession of the place, and, bringing his lawyer with him, had taken up his abode in the house, waiting impatiently for the old man's death to sell up everything, for he held a mortgage on the stock and furniture.

The first thing he did was to shut up the shop; and having looked out from among the old furniture the handsomest and most comfortable chair he could find for his own use, and an especially uncomfortable one for the use of the lawyer, he had them carried into the little back parlour, where he took up his abode to be on the spot when the old man died.

Upstairs, Nelly watched by the old man's pillow, listening to him whispering her name in his delirium, and crying out in his feverish wanderings that he had ruined her.

"Aha! Nelly, how is he now, my duck of diamonds?" asked the dwarf, as she timidly stole downstairs; for she had avoided the back parlour as much as possible.

"He's very bad," replied the weeping child.

"Has she come to sit on Quilp's knee?" said the dwarf, "or is she going to bed in her own little room inside here? Which is poor Nelly going to do?"

"I am not going to stay at all," faltered Nell. "I want a few things out of that room, and then I—I—won't come down here any more."

"And a very nice little room it is!" said the dwarf, looking into it as Nelly entered. "Quite a bower. You're sure you're not going to use it; you're sure you're not coming back, Nelly?"

"No," replied the child, hurrying away with the few articles of dress she had come to remove; "never again, never again!"

"She's very sensitive," said Quilp, looking after her. "very sensitive; that's a pity. The bedstead is just about my size. I think I shall make it *my* little room." And the dwarf, walking in, threw himself on his back upon the bed with his pipe in his mouth, and, finding it soft and comfortable, remained where he was till he had smoked his pipe out.

Nelly shrank timidly from all the dwarfs advances towards conversation, and fled from the very sound of his voice; she knew he was getting more impatient every day for the old man's death; and he still lingered.

One night she had stolen to her usual window—the window where she had often sat watching the stars when the old man had gone off to his nightly haunt— and was sitting there very sorrowfully, when she thought she heard her name called softly by a voice in the street, and, looking down, she recognised Kit.

"I have wanted to say a word to you for a long time," said Kit, "but the people below have driven me away and wouldn't let me see you. You don't believe —I hope you don't really believe—that I deserve to be cast off as I have been; do you, Miss?"

"I must believe it," said Nelly; "or why would Grandfather have been so angry with you?"

"I don't know," replied Kit; "I'm sure I've never deserved it from him; no, nor from you. I can say that with a true and honest heart, anyway. And then to be driven from the door when I only came to ask how old Master was!"

"They never told me that," said Nell. "I didn't know it, indeed. I wouldn't have had them do it for the world."

"Thankee, Miss," said Kit; "it's comfortable to hear you say that. I said I would never believe that it was your doing."

"That was right," said Nell eagerly.

"Miss Nell," said the boy, coming under the window and speaking in a lower tone, "there are new masters downstairs. It's a change for you."

"It is, indeed," said the child.

"And so it will be for him when he gets better," said Kit, pointing to the sickroom.

"If he ever does," added Nell, unable to restrain her tears.

"Oh, he'll do that, he'll do that," said Kit. "I am sure he will. You mustn't be cast down, Miss Nell."

His encouragement and consoling words so affected the child that she only wept the more.

"He'll be sure to get better now," said Kit anxiously, "if you don't give way to low spirits and turn ill yourself, which would make him worse and throw him back just as he was recovering. When he does, say a good word—say a kind word for me, Miss Nell."

"They tell me that I must not even mention your name to him for a long, long time," rejoined Nelly. "I dare not, and, even if I might, what good would a kind word do you, Kit? We shall be very poor. We shall scarcely have bread to eat."

"It's not that I might be taken back," said the boy, "that I ask the favour of you. It isn't for the sake of food and wages that I have been waiting about so long in hopes to see you. Don't think that I'd come in a time of trouble to talk of such things as them."

Nell looked gratefully and kindly at him, but waited that he might speak again.

"No, it is not that," said Kit, hesitating; "it's something very different from that;—well then—it is this," cried Kit with sudden boldness. "This home is gone from you and him. Mother and I have got a poor one, but that's better than this with all these people here; and why not come there till he's had time to look about and find a better?"

Nelly was so much affected that she could not speak.

"You think," said Kit, "that it's very small and inconvenient. So it is, but it's very clean. The little front room upstairs is very pleasant. You can see a piece of the church clock through the chimneys, and almost tell the time; Mother says it would be just the thing for you, and so it would, and you'd have her to wait upon you both, and me to run of errands. We don't mean money, bless you; you're not to think of that. Will you try him, Miss Nell? Only say you'll try him. Do try to make old Master come, and ask him first what I've done—will you only promise that, Miss Nell?"

Before Nelly could reply the street door opened, and Mr Brass the lawyer, thrusting out his night-capped head, called in a surly voice, "Who is there?"

Kit immediately glided away, and Nell, closing the window softly, drew back into the room, her affectionate heart touched to the quick by the kind and generous spirit of her old favourite Kit.

6

Leaving the Old Home

At last the crisis of the old man's fever was past and he began to mend. By very slow and feeble degrees his consciousness came back, but his mind was very weak. He was patient and quiet; and would sit for hours with Nell's small hand in his, playing with her fingers, and stopping sometimes to smooth her hair or kiss her brow.

They went out sometimes for a drive; the old man propped up with pillows, and Nell beside him. He was not surprised, or curious, or pleased, or irritated with anything. He was just placid.

He was sitting in his easy chair one day, and Nell upon a stool beside him, when somebody outside the door inquired if he might enter. "Yes," said the old man quietly. It was Quilp, he knew. Quilp was master there. Of course he might come in.

"I'm glad to see you well again at last, neighbour," said the dwarf, sitting down opposite him. "You're quite strong now."

"Yes," said the old man feebly, "yes."

"I don't want to hurry you, neighbour," said the dwarf, "but as soon as you *can* arrange your future proceedings, the better."

"Surely," said the old man. "The better for all parties."

"You see," said Quilp, "the goods being once removed, this house would be uncomfortable."

"You say true," said the old man. "Poor Nell, too, what would *she* do?"

"Exactly," said the dwarf, "that is very well observed. Then will you consider about it, neighbour?"

"I will certainly," replied the old man. "We shall not stop here."

"So I supposed," said the dwarf. "I have sold the things. They have not yielded quite as much as they might have done, but pretty well—pretty well. Today is Tuesday. When shall they be moved? There's no hurry—shall we say this afternoon?"

"Say Friday morning," said the old man.

"Very good," said the dwarf. "So be it—with the understanding that I can't go beyond that day, neighbour, on any account."

"Good," returned the old man, "I shall remember it."

The dwarf was puzzled that he should take it so quietly. He did not understand it.

All that day, and all the next, the old man wandered up and down the house, and in and out of the familiar rooms, as if he was bidding them goodbye, whispering to Nelly to be of good-cheer, saying that they would not desert each other.

Thursday arrived, and then a change came upon him towards the evening, as he and Nelly sat silently together.

"It has come back upon me today; it has all come back since we have been sitting here," said the old man, with tears in his eyes. "I bless thee for it, Nell!"

"For what, dear Grandfather?"

"For what you said when we were first made beggars, Nell. Let us speak softly. Hush! for if they knew our purpose downstairs, they would cry that I was mad, and take thee from me. We will not stop here another day. We will go far away from here."

"Yes, let us go," said Nelly earnestly; "let us be gone from this place, and never turn back or think of it again."

"We will," answered the old man, "we will travel afoot through fields and woods, and by the side of rivers, and trust ourselves to God in places where He dwells. It is far better to lie down at night beneath an open sky than to rest in close rooms which are always full of care and weary dreams. Thou and I together, Nell, may be cheerful and happy yet, and learn to forget this time, as if it had never been."

"We will be happy," cried the child. "We never can be here."

"No, we never can again—never again—that's truly said. Let us steal away together tomorrow morning— early and softly, that we may not be seen and heard—and leave no trace or track for them to follow by. Poor Nell, thy cheek is pale, and thy eyes are heavy with watching and weeping; but thou wilt be well again, and merry, too, when we are far away. Tomorrow morning, dear, we'll turn our faces from this scene of sorrow, and be as free and happy as the birds."

Nelly's heart beat high with hope and confidence. She had no thought of hunger, or cold, or thirst, or suffering. She saw in this but a return of the simple pleasures they had once enjoyed, and a life of tranquil happiness.

The old man had slept for some hours soundly in his bed, and Nell was yet busily engaged in preparing for their flight. There were a few articles of clothing for herself to carry and a few for him; and a staff to support his feeble steps put ready for his use. And then she went round to visit the old rooms for the last time.

It was hard not to be able to glance round her own little room once more—her little room where she had so often knelt and prayed at night. There were some trifles there that she would have liked to take away; but that was impossible, for Quilp was sleeping there.

This brought to mind her bird, her poor bird that hung there yet, and she wept for the loss of this little creature as she crept to her bed to rest.

At length the day began to glimmer, and the stars to grow pale and dim. As soon as she was sure of this, she rose and dressed herself for the journey.

The old man was anxious that they should leave the house without a minute's loss of time, and was soon ready.

Nelly then took him by the hand, and they crept cautiously down the stairs, trembling whenever a board creaked, and often stopping to listen. At last they reached the passage on the ground floor where the snoring of the dwarf and Mr Brass sounded more terrible in their ears than the roars of lions. The bolts of the door were rusty, and difficult to unfasten without noise. When they were all drawn back it was found to be locked, and, worst of all, the key was gone; and Nell remembered, for the first time, one of the nurses having told her that Quilp always locked both the house doors at night, and kept the keys on the table in his bedroom.

In fear and trembling Nelly slipped off her shoes, and gliding through the store-room of old curiosities, where Mr Brass lay sleeping on a mattress, she passed into her own little room. Here she stood for a few moments quite transfixed with terror at the sight of Mr Quilp, who was hanging half out of her little bed, gasping and growling with his mouth wide open.

With a hasty glance round the room Nelly secured the

key and rejoined the old man in safety, and put her shoes on again. They got the door open without noise, and passing into the street, stood still.

"Which way?" said the child.

The old man looked helplessly first at her, then to the right and left, then at her again, and shook his head. It was plain that *she* thenceforth was to be his guide and leader; and, putting her hand in his, Nelly led him gently away.

Forth from the city, while it yet slumbered, went the two poor adventurers, wandering they knew not whither.

7

A Disappointed Visitor

The dwarf slept on, and Mr Brass still snored, unconscious of their flight, when there came a modest rap at the front door. It was too gentle to wake the sleepers. And then, suddenly, the gentle rap was followed by a perfect battery of loud knocks, which grew louder and louder; and Quilp, awakening, remembered at once that this was Friday morning, the day the furniture was to be removed, and that he had ordered Mrs Quilp to be in waiting upon him at an early hour.

The noise woke the lawyer as well, and the two men struggled into their clothes as fast as they could.

"What's the matter?" asked Brass, for Mr Quilp was groping under the table and muttering curses to himself.

"The key," said the dwarf, "the door-key—that's the matter. D'ye know anything of it?"

Mr Brass suggested that it might have been left in the door over night; and although Mr Quilp felt certain that he had brought it away with him as usual, he went grumbling to the door, where, sure enough, he found it.

Now, just as Mr Quilp laid his hand upon the lock, and saw with great astonishment that the bolts were all drawn, the knocking came again with irritating violence. It exasperated the dwarf, and he determined to dart out suddenly and punish Mrs Quilp for daring to make such an uproar.

So he turned the handle very softly, and, opening the door all at once, pounced out upon the person on the other side, who at that moment raised the knocker to thunder again, and at whom the dwarf ran head first, flinging out his hands, and biting the air in his malice.

Mr Quilp was no sooner in the arms of the individual whom he had taken for his wife, than he found himself received with two staggering blows on the head, and two more of the same quality in the chest. He closed with his assailant; but such a shower of blows rained down upon his person that he was convinced immediately that he was in skilful and experienced hands.

The dwarf clung tight to the leg of his opponent, and bit and hammered away with such heartiness that it was at least a couple of minutes before he was dislodged, when he found himself, all flushed and dishevelled, in the middle of the street with a young man, of the name of Dick Swiveller, performing a kind of dance around him, and requiring to know "whether he wanted any more?"

"There's plenty more of it at the same shop," said Mr Swiveller, in a threatening attitude. "Will you have a little more, sir—don't say no, if you'd rather not."

"I thought it was somebody else," said Quilp, rubbing his shoulders; "why didn't you say who you were?"

"Why didn't you say who *you* were?" returned Dick, "instead of flying out of the house like a Bedlamite?"

"It was you that—that knocked," said the dwarf, getting up with a short groan, "was it?"

"Yes, I am the man," replied Mr Swiveller. "That lady

had begun when I came, but she knocked too soft, so I relieved her." As he said this he pointed towards Mrs Quilp, who stood trembling at a little distance.

"Humph!" muttered the dwarf, darting an angry look at his wife, "I thought it was your fault! And you, sir, what is it that you want?"

"I want to know how the old gentleman is, and to hear from Nell herself, with whom I should like to have a little talk. I'm a friend of the family, Sir—at least, I'm a friend of one of the family, and that's the same thing."

"You'd better walk in, then," said the dwarf. "Now, Mrs Quilp," he added, when they had entered the shop, "go upstairs, if you please, to Nelly's room, and tell her that she's wanted."

"You seem to make yourself at home here," said Mr Swiveller, staring at the dwarf.

"I am at home, young gentleman," said Mr Quilp.

And then Mrs Quilp came hurrying downstairs declaring that the rooms above were empty.

"Empty, you fool!" said Quilp.

"I give you my word, Quilp," answered his trembling wife, "that I have been into every room and there's not a soul in any of them!"

"And that," said Mr Brass, clapping his hands together, "explains the mystery of the key."

Quilp looked frowningly round, and, hurrying upstairs, soon hurried down again, for he had found the rooms empty too.

"It's a strange way of going," said the dwarf; "very strange not to communicate with me who am such a close and intimate friend of his! Ah! he'll write to me, no doubt, or he'll bid Nelly write—yes, yes, that's what he'll do. Nelly's very fond of me. Pretty Nell!"

Mr Swiveller was too much astonished to speak. And

Quilp, turning to the lawyer, said that this need not interfere with the removal of the furniture.

"We knew that they'd go away today," he added, "but not that they'd go so early or so quietly."

"Where are they gone?" asked the wondering Dick.

Quilp shook his head, and pursed up his lips as if to say he knew very well but was not at liberty to tell.

"And what," said Mr Swiveller, looking at the confusion about him, "what do you mean by moving the goods?"

"That I have bought 'em, Sir," rejoined Quilp. "Eh? What then?"

Dick Swiveller was utterly aghast at the whole affair.

He was a friend of Nelly's scapegrace brother, Fred, who, quite sure that his old grandfather was a wealthy miser, had made up a pretty little plan with Mr Swiveller. It was that Dick should make himself so charming to Nelly that he might win her heart, so that when she was old enough he could marry her, and so come in for all the money that the old miser had stored away.

"You'll mention that I called, perhaps?" said Dick.

Mr Quilp said he certainly would, the very first time he saw them; and bade him good day.

In his secret heart the dwarf was surprised and troubled by the flight of the old man. He was sure he had some secret store of money, that he knew nothing about, with which he had run away; and the bare idea of its escaping his clutches overwhelmed Mr Quilp with mortification.

By this time the vans for removing the furniture had arrived, and Mr Quilp went to work with surprising vigour, hustling and bustling everybody about like an evil spirit, so that no time was lost; and in a few hours the whole house was empty of everything but pieces of matting, and scattered fragments of straw.

The dwarf was regaling himself in the parlour with bread and cheese and beer, when he observed that a boy was prying in at the outer door.

"Come here, you sir," said the dwarf, as soon as he saw it was Kit. "Well, so your old master and young mistress have gone?"

"Where?" said Kit, looking round.

"You mean to say you don't know where?" answered Quilp sharply. "Where have they gone, eh?"

"I don't know," said Kit.

"Come," retorted Quilp, "let's have no more of this. Do you mean to say that you don't know they went away by stealth, as soon as it was light this morning?"

"No," said Kit, in evident surprise.

And then the boy from the wharf, who had been skulking about in search of anything that might have been left about by accident, cried out, "Here's a bird! What's to be done with this?"

"Wring its neck," said Quilp.

"No, no, don't do that," said Kit, stepping forward; "give it to me."

"Oh! yes, I dare say," said the boy from the wharf. "Come! you let the cage alone, and let me wring its neck, will you? He said I was to do it. You let the cage alone, will you?"

"Give it here, give it to me, you dogs," roared Quilp. "Fight for it, you dogs, or I'll wring its neck myself."

In an instant the boys fell upon each other, tooth and nail, while Quilp, holding up the cage in one hand, urged them on by his taunts and cries to fight more fiercely. They were a pretty equal match, and rolled about together, exchanging blows which were by no means child's play, until at length Kit, planting a well directed hit in his adversary's chest, disengaged himself, sprang nimbly up, and snatching the cage from Quilp's hands, made off with his prize.

He did not stop until he reached home, where his bleeding face made his mother cry out.

"Goodness gracious, Kit, what's the matter? What have you been doing?"

"Never you mind, mother. I'm not hurt; don't you be afraid for me. I've been fighting for a bird! And here he is—Miss Nelly's bird, Mother, that they were going to wring the neck of. I stopped that though—ha, ha, ha! They wouldn't wring his neck, and me by, no, no. It wouldn't do, Mother, it wouldn't do at all. Ha, ha, ha!"

And then he hung the cage up in the window; and told his mother that he would go out and see if he could find a horse to hold. "And then I can buy some seed," he added; and away he ran.

8

The Wanderers

The fugitives, often pressing each other's hands, or exchanging a smile or cheerful look, went on their way in silence through the long deserted streets.

Nelly trembled sometimes in mingled hope and fear when she saw, in the distance, some figure which looked like honest Kit's. She would have liked to thank him for what he had said at their last meeting; but she dreaded the effect which the sight of him might have on the poor old man, who believed it was Kit who had betrayed his secret to the dwarf, and through whom all his trouble and illness had come about; so it was always a relief to find that the figure that looked like Kit's was not his when it came nearer, but a stranger's.

After a while some straggling carts and coaches rumbled by; then others came, and then a crowd. Smoke rose slowly from the chimneys, and window sashes were thrown up to let in air, and doors were opened, and servant-maids looked out, and listened to milkmen who spoke of country fairs.

On, on they trudged, until they came upon the busy streets where people were hurrying to their work from every side.

By degrees they left the town behind, and came at length upon the open fields. Then came a turnpike; then fields again with trees and haystacks. And here the old man and his little guide (if guide she were who knew not whither they were bound) sat down to rest. Nelly had furnished her basket with some slices of bread and meat, and here they made their breakfast.

The freshness of the day, the singing of the birds, the beauty of the waving grass, and the thousand exquisite scents and sounds that floated in the air, sank into their breasts and made them very glad.

She had said her prayers before they had left home that morning more earnestly, perhaps, than she had ever done before in all her life; and as she looked round, and felt how calm and beautiful it was, she said her prayers again, in the thankfulness of her heart, and the old man, pulling off his hat, said "Amen" at the end.

"Are you tired?" said Nelly; "are you sure you don't feel ill from this long walk?"

"I shall never feel ill again, now that we are once away. Let us be stirring, Nell. We must be further away—a long, long way further. We are too near to stop, and be at rest. Come!"

There was a pool of clear water in the field, in which Nelly washed her hands and face, and cooled her feet before setting forth to walk again, helping the old man to refresh himself as well.

"I can do nothing for myself, my darling," said the grandfather. "I don't know how it is; I could once, but the time is gone. Don't leave me, Nell; say that thou wilt not leave me. I loved thee all the while, indeed I did. If I lose thee too, I must die."

He laid his head on her shoulder and moaned piteously. Nell soothed him with gentle, tender words, and smiled at his thinking they could ever part. She could not weep with him; the time for tears was past; she was to be his guide, his consoler, his protector now, she knew. He was soon calmed and fell asleep, singing to himself in a low voice, like a little child.

He awoke refreshed, and they continued their journey. The road was pleasant, for they were now in the open country; the houses were very few, and often miles apart, and occasionally they came upon a cluster of cottages. They walked all day, and slept that night at a small cottage where beds were let to travellers. Next morning they were afoot again, often stopping to rest, but only for a short space at a time.

It was nearly five o'clock in the afternoon, when, drawing near another cluster of labourers' huts, Nell looked wistfully in each, wondering where she might ask for permission to rest awhile, and buy a draught of milk.

At length she stopped at one where the family were seated round the table—chiefly because there was an old man sitting in a cushioned chair beside the hearth, and she thought he was a grandfather and would feel for hers.

Nell timidly asked if they might rest awhile and buy a little milk, and her request was immediately granted. The eldest boy ran out to fetch some milk, the second dragged two stools towards the door, and the youngest crept to his mother's gown, and peeped at the strangers from beneath his sunburnt hands.

"God save you, Master," said the old cottager, in a thin piping voice; "are you travelling far?"

"Yes, Sir, a long way," answered Nelly, for her grandfather.

"From London?" inquired the old cottager.

Nell said, "Yes."

"Sit thee down, Master, in the elbow chair," urged he. "Take a pinch out of that box. I don't take much myself, for it comes dear; but I find it wakes me up sometimes, and ye're but a boy to me."

The milk arrived, and Nelly producing her basket, and selecting its best fragments for her grandfather, they made a hearty meal.

"How far is it to any town or village?" Nelly asked.

"A matter of good five mile, my dear, but you're not going on tonight?"

"Yes, yes, Nell," said the old man hurriedly, urging her, too, by signs. "Further on, further on, darling, further away if we walk till midnight."

"There's a good barn hard by, Master," said the man. "Excuse me, but you do seem a little tired, and unless you're anxious to get on—"

"Yes, yes, we are!" cried the old man fretfully.

"We must go on, indeed," said Nelly, yielding to his restless wish. "We thank you very much, but we cannot stop so soon. I'm quite ready, Grandfather."

But the woman had observed that one of Nelly's little feet was sore and blistered, and she would not suffer her to go until she had washed the place and applied some simple remedy, which she did so carefully and with such a gentle hand—rough-grained and hard though it was with work—that the child's heart was too full to let her say more than, "God bless you," fervently.

The wanderers trudged forward, more slowly and painfully than they had done yet, for another mile or so, when they heard the sound of wheels behind them, and looking round they saw an empty cart approaching briskly. The driver, on coming up to them, stopped his horse and looked earnestly at Nell.

"Didn't you stop to rest at a cottage yonder?" he said.

Nelly said, "Yes."

"Ah! They asked me to look out for you," said the man. "I'm going your way. Give me your hand—jump up, Master."

This was a great relief, for they were very tired.

To them the jolting of the cart was a luxurious carriage, and the ride the most delicious in the world. Nelly had scarcely settled herself on a little heap of straw on one corner, when she fell asleep, and was awakened by the stopping of the cart, which was about to turn up a narrow lane.

The driver kindly got down to help her out, and pointing to some trees at a very short distance before them, said that the town lay there, and that they had better take the path which they would see leading through the churchyard.

The sun was setting when they reached the wicket gate at which the path began, and soon they gained the churchyard and the old grey church with ivy clinging to the walls.

Here they quitted the gravel path, and strayed among the tombs, for there the ground was soft and easy to their tired feet. As they passed behind the church, they heard voices near at hand, and presently came upon two men who were sitting on the grass, and so busily engaged that they did not see the newcomers.

It was not difficult to discern that they were the travelling showmen of a Punch-and-Judy Show; for Punch himself was perched cross-legged upon a tombstone, his nose and chin as hooked, and his face as beaming as usual; and scattered upon the ground at the feet of the two men were Judy and the Baby, the Doctor and the Hangman, and the other figures belonging to the Punch-and-Judy Show.

Their owners had evidently come to that spot to make some needful repairs, for one of them was engaged in binding together a small gallows with thread, while the other was fixing a new black wig, with the aid of a small hammer and some tacks, upon the head of one of the dolls.

They raised their eyes when Nell and the old man were close upon them, and, pausing in their work, stared curiously. One of them—the showman, no doubt—was a little merry-faced man with a twinkling eye and a red nose. The other—the one that took the money—had a careful and cautious look.

The merry little man greeted the strangers with a nod, and following the old man's eyes, he remarked that perhaps that was the first time he had ever seen a Punch off the stage.

"Why do you come here to do this?" said the old man, sitting down beside them, and looking at the figures with extreme delight.

"Why, you see," said the merry man, "we're putting up for tonight at a public-house yonder, and it wouldn't do to let 'em see the present company undergoing repair."

"Look here," said the cautious man, whose name was Codlin, "here's all this Judy's clothes falling to pieces again. You haven't got a needle and thread, I suppose?"

The merry man shook his head, and scratched it ruefully.

Seeing that they were at a loss, Nelly said, timidly, "I have a needle, Sir, in my basket, and thread too. Will you let me try to mend it for you? I think I could do it neater than you could."

Even the cautious Codlin had nothing against such a welcome proposal; and Nelly, kneeling down beside the dolls, was soon busily engaged in her task, and accomplished it beautifully.

The merry little man looked at her with much interest, and then at her helpless companion. When she had finished her work he thanked her, and inquired whither they were travelling.

"No—no further tonight, I think," said Nelly, looking towards her grandfather.

"If you're wanting a place to stop at," said the merry man, "I should advise you to take up at the same house with us. That's it—the long, low, white house there. It's very cheap."

The old man was so childishly delighted with the dolls that he gave his willing consent, and they all rose and walked away together.

The public-house was kept by a fat old landlord and landlady, who made no objection to receiving their new guests, and were so pleased with Nelly's beauty that they took to her at once.

"These two gentlemen have ordered supper in an hour's time," said the landlady, taking Nell into the bar, "and your best plan will be to sup with them. Meantime you shall have a little taste of something that'll do you good, for I'm sure you must be wanting it after all you've gone through today. Now, don't look after the old gentleman, because, when you've drunk that, he shall have some too."

When they had been thus refreshed, the whole house hurried away into an empty stable where the show stood, and where the showmen were going to begin a performance before the inmates of the house.

It was a great success, and everything was highly applauded. Among the laughter none was more loud and frequent than the old man's. Nell's was unheard; for she, poor child, with her head drooping on his shoulder, had fallen asleep, and slept too soundly to be roused.

The supper was very good, but Nelly was too tired to eat; and yet she would not leave the old man until she had kissed him in his bed. He, happily insensible to every care and anxiety, sat listening with a vacant smile to all his new friends said; and it was not until they retired yawning to their room, that he followed the child upstairs.

It was only a loft partitioned into two compartments where they were to rest, but they were well pleased with their lodging, and had hoped for none so good.

And when she left her grandfather, Nell sat upon the bed, and thought of the life that was before them.

She had a little money, but it was very little, and when that was gone they must begin to beg. There was one piece of gold among it, and a time might come when they might want it badly. It would be best to hide this piece of gold, and never produce it unless their case was desperate, and no other resource was left them.

So Nelly sewed the piece of gold into her dress, and going to bed with a lighter heart sank into a deep slumber.

9

On the Way to the Races

Another bright day was shining in through the small casement when Nelly awoke, and started up in alarm at the sight of the strange room and its unaccustomed objects. But another glance round called to her mind all that had lately passed, and she sprang from her bed, hoping and trustful.

"And where are you going today?" asked Short, addressing himself to Nell, as they ate their breakfast together.

"Indeed, I hardly know—we have not determined yet," replied Nelly.

"We're going on to the races," said the merry man. "If that's your way, and you like to have us for company, let us travel together. If you prefer going alone, only say the word and you'll find that we shan't trouble you."

"We'll go with you," put in the old man. "Nell,—with them, with them."

Nelly considered for a moment, and thinking that she must shortly beg, and could scarcely hope to do so at a better place than where crowds of rich ladies and gentlemen were assembled, determined to accompany the Punch-and-Judy showmen so far. She therefore thanked the merry man for his offer, and said, glancing timidly towards his cautious friend, that if there was no objection to their accompanying them as far as the race town

"Objection!" broke in Short. "Now, be gracious for once, Tommy, and say that you'd rather they went with us. I know you would. Be gracious, Tommy."

"Short," said Mr Codlin, who talked very slowly and ate very greedily, "you're too free."

"Why, what harm can it do?" cried Short.

"No harm at all in this particular case, perhaps," growled Codlin; "but the principle's a dangerous one, and you're too free, I tell you."

"Well, are they to go with us or not?"

"Yes, they are," said Codlin; "but you might have made a favour of it, mightn't you?"

Short tried to cheer his discontented friend with a merry joke, and applied himself with great relish to the cold boiled beef, the tea, and the bread and butter; and urged Nelly and the old man strongly to do the same.

Codlin then called for the bill, and Nelly paying her share, which Codlin took care should be exactly half, they bade farewell to the landlord and landlady, and resumed their journey together.

The day was sultry, and the dust lay thick upon the road. Short led the way with the long flat box which contained the dolls, and a brass trumpet slung over his shoulder. Nell and her grandfather walked next him on either hand; and Mr Codlin, trudging heavily along, and carrying on his shoulders Punch's theatre or stage, brought up the rear, stopping to rest and growl occasionally at its weight.

When they came to any town or village, or even to a detached house of good appearance, Short blew a blast upon the brazen trumpet. If people hurried to the windows, Mr Codlin pitched the stage directly, and the performance began at once.

Sometimes they played out the toll across a bridge or ferry, and once a drunken turnpike keeper paid down a shilling to have the performance to himself.

They made a long day's journey, notwithstanding these interruptions, and were still upon the road when the moon was shining in the sky. The merry man beguiled the time with songs and jests, and made the best of everything that happened.

Mr Codlin, on the other hand, limped along with the theatre on his back, with a very sulky face. They stopped to rest beneath a finger-post where four roads met, when Codlin declared that he would put up at *The Jolly Sandboys,* and nowhere else that night.

"If you like to come there," he said to Short, "come there. If you like to go on by yourself, go on by yourself, and do without me if you can."

So saying, he took the theatre on his shoulders with a jerk, and made off with the most remarkable speed.

Short then hastened to follow his surly partner, and giving his unoccupied hand to Nell, bade her be of good cheer, as they would soon be at the end of their journey for that night.

The Jolly Sandboys was a small and very ancient roadside inn on the way to the race town, and as the travellers had observed gipsy camps, and showmen of various kinds, and beggars and tramps of every degree, all wending their way in the same direction, Mr Codlin was fearful of finding the inn too full to receive them; so he quickened his pace and never stopped till he reached the threshold.

He found the landlord leaning against the door-post,

looking lazily at the rain, which by this time had begun to fall; and his attitude calmed Mr Codlin's fears.

"All alone?" said Mr Codlin, putting down his burden and wiping his forehead.

"All alone as yet," rejoined the landlord, glancing at the sky, "but we shall have more company tonight, I expect. Here, one of you boys, carry that show into the barn. Make haste in out of the wet, Tom; when it came on to rain I told 'em to make up the fire, and there's a glorious blaze in the kitchen, I can tell you."

Mr Codlin followed with a willing mind, and found a mighty fire blazing on the hearth and roaring up the wide chimney with a cheerful sound, with a large iron pot bubbling and simmering in the heat.

There was a deep red ruddy blush upon the room; and when the landlord stirred the fire, sending the flame skipping and leaping up—when he took off the lid of the iron pot and there rushed out a savoury smell, while the bubbling sound grew deeper, and a rich steam came floating out hanging in a delicious mist over their heads—when he did this, Mr Codlin's heart was touched. He sat down in the chimney corner and smiled; and, drawing his sleeve across his lips, he said in a murmuring voice, "What is it?"

"It's a stew of tripe," said the landlord, smacking his lips, "and cow-heel," smacking them again, "and bacon," smacking them once more, "and steak," smacking them for the fourth time, "and peas, cauliflowers, new potatoes, and sparrow-grass, all working up together in one delicious gravy."

Then he smacked his lips a great many times and, taking a long hearty sniff of the fragrance that was hovering about, put on the cover again with the air of one whose toils on earth are over.

"At what time will it be ready?" asked Mr Codlin faintly.

"It'll be done to a turn," said the landlord looking at the clock; "it'll be done to a turn at twenty-two minutes before eleven."

"Then," said Mr Codlin, "fetch me a pint of warm ale, and don't let nobody bring into the room even so much as a biscuit till the time arrives."

The rain was rattling against the windows and pouring down in torrents; but Mr Codlin felt so amiable as he drank his warm ale, that he said more than once that he hoped the others wouldn't get wet.

They came at last, drenched with rain and looking miserable, though Short had sheltered Nell as well as he could under the skirts of his own coat; and they were nearly breathless with the haste they had made.

But the landlord, who had been on the look-out for their coming, rushed into the kitchen and took the cover off the pot; and though the wet was dripping from their clothes upon the floor, they all came in with smiling faces, and Short's first remark was, "What a delicious smell!"

They were soon furnished with slippers and such dry garments as the house or their own bundles afforded, and, taking their places in the warm chimney corner, they forgot their late troubles as easily as Codlin had done. Overpowered by the warmth and comfort, and the fatigue they had undergone, Nell and the old man soon fell asleep.

"Who are they?" whispered the landlord.

Short shook his head, and said he wished he knew himself.

"Don't you know?" asked the host, turning Mr Codlin.

"Not I," he replied. "They're no good, I suppose."

"They're no harm," said Short. "Depend upon that. I

tell you what—it's plain that the old man ain't in his right mind."

"If you haven't got anything newer than that to say," growled Mr Codlin, glancing at the clock, "you'd better let us fix our minds upon the supper, and not disturb us."

"Hear me out, won't you?" retorted his friend. "It's very plain to me, besides, that they are not used to this way of life. Don't tell me that that handsome child has been in the habit of prowling about as she's done these last two or three days. I know better. Have you seen how anxious the old man is to get on—always wanting to be furder away—furder away? Have you seen that?"

"Ah! what then?" muttered Mr Codlin.

"This, then," said Short. "He has given his friends the slip, and persuaded this delicate young creature all along of her fondness for him to be his guide and travelling companion—where to, he knows no more than the man in the moon. Now, I'm not a-going to stand that."

"*You're* not going to stand that!" cried Mr Codlin, glancing at the clock again. "Here's a world to live in!"

"I," repeated Short slowly, "am not a-going to stand it. I'm not a-going to see this fair young child a-falling into bad hands, and getting among people that she's no more fit for than they are to get among angels as their ordinary chums. Therefore, when they dewelope an intention of parting company from us, I shall take measures for detaining of 'em, and restoring 'em to their friends, who, I dare say, have had their disconsolation posted up on every wall in London, by this time."

"Short," said Mr Codlin, who had been shaking himself impatiently, but who now looked up with eager eyes, "it's possible there may be uncommon sense in that you've said. If there is, and there should be a reward, Short, remember that we're partners in everything."

Short had only time to nod assent, for Nell awoke at the instant; and strange footsteps were heard without, and fresh company entered.

These were no other than four very dismal dogs that came pattering in one after the other, headed by an old bandy dog that erected itself upon its hind legs and looked round at his companions, who immediately stood upon their hind legs in a grave and melancholy row. They each wore a kind of little coat of some gaudy colour trimmed with tarnished spangles, which were wet through and discoloured with rain.

Neither Short, nor the landlord, nor Mr Codlin, however, was the least surprised; merely remarking that these were Jerry's dogs, and that Jerry could not be far behind. The dogs stood patiently winking and looking extremely hard at the boiling pot, until Jerry himself appeared, when they all dropped down at once and walked about the room in their ordinary manner.

Jerry, the manager of these dancing dogs, was a tall, black-whiskered man in a velveteen coat, who seemed well known to the landlord and his guests, and met them with great cordiality. He put down a barrel organ which he carried, but kept in his hand a little whip as he came up to the fire to dry himself.

"Your people don't usually travel in character, do they?" said Short, pointing to the dresses of the dogs. "It must come expensive if they do?"

"No," replied Jerry, "it's not the custom with us. But we've been playing a little on the road today, and we come out with a new wardrobe at the races, so I didn't think it was worth while to stop and undress."

The landlord now busied himself in laying the cloth; and Mr Codlin, obligingly setting his own knife and fork in the most convenient place, sat down behind them.

When everything was ready the landlord took the cover off the pot for the last time, and a stout servant-maid helped him to turn the contents into a large tureen; a proceeding which the dogs watched with terrible eagerness. The great dish having been lifted on the table, little Nell ventured to say grace, and supper began.

The poor dogs immediately stood on their hind legs, and Nell, having pity on them, was about to cast some morsels of food to them before she tasted it herself, when their master interposed.

"No, my dear, not an atom from anybody's hand but mine, if you please. That dog," said Jerry, pointing out the old leader of the troop and speaking in a terrible voice, "lost a ha'penny today. *He* goes without his supper."

The unfortunate dog dropped upon his fore legs directly, wagged his tail, and looked imploringly at his master.

"You must be more careful, Sir," said Jerry, walking coolly to the chair where he had placed the organ, and setting the stop. "Come here, sir. Now you play away at that while we have supper, and leave off if you dare."

The dog immediately began to grind most mournful music. His master, having shown him the whip, resumed his seat and called up the others, who, at his directions, formed in a row, standing upright as a file of soldiers.

"Now, gentlemen," said Jerry, looking at them attentively, "the dog whose name's called, eats. The dogs whose names an't called, keep quiet. Carlo!"

The lucky dog whose name was called snapped up the morsel thrown to him, but none of the others moved a muscle. In this manner they were fed by their master. Meanwhile, the dog in disgrace ground hard at the organ—sometimes in quick time, sometimes in slow, but never leaving off for an instant. When the knives and forks rattled very much, or when any of his fellows got an unusually large piece of fat, he accompanied the music with a short howl, but checked it immediately on his master looking round, and applied himself more diligently to the tune of the Old Hundredth.

10

"Codlin's the Friend "

When supper was over, the weary child prevailed upon her grandfather to retire; and they withdrew, leaving the company yet seated round the fire, and the dogs fast asleep at a humble distance. After bidding the old man good night Nelly retired to her little garret, but had scarcely closed the door when it was gently tapped upon.

She opened it directly, and was a little startled to see Mr Codlin, whom she had left to all appearance fast asleep downstairs.

"What is the matter?" said Nell.

"Nothing's the matter, my dear," returned her visitor. "I'm your friend. Perhaps you haven't thought so, but it's me that's your friend—not him."

"Not who?" said Nell.

"Short, my dear. I tell you what," said Codlin, "for all his having a kind of way with him that you'd be very apt to like, I'm the real, open-hearted man. I mayn't look it, but I am indeed."

Nelly began to feel alarmed, thinking that the ale had taken effect upon Mr Codlin.

"Short's very well, and seems kind," went on Codlin, "but he overdoes it. Now I don't."

73

Nelly was very much puzzled, and couldn't tell what to say.

"Take my advice," said Mr Codlin; "don't ask me why, but take it. As long as you can travel with us, keep as near me as you can. Don't offer to leave us—on no account—but always stick to me, and say I'm your friend. Will you bear that in mind, my dear, and always say that it was me that was your friend?"

"Say so where—and when?" asked Nelly innocently.

"Oh, nowhere in particular," replied Codlin, a little put out by the question. "I'm only anxious that you should think me so, and do me justice. You can't think what an interest I have in you. I think they are breaking up downstairs; you needn't tell Short, you know, that we've had this little talk together. God bless you. Recollect the friend. Codlin's the friend, not Short. Short's very well, as far as he goes, but the real friend is Codlin—not Short."

Mr Codlin stole away on tiptoe, leaving Nell very much surprised. She was still thinking why he should suddenly be so anxious to be thought her friend—for, truth to tell, Mr Codlin hadn't taken any pains to be friendly before—when the stairs creaked beneath the tread of the other travellers who were passing to their beds.

When the sound of their footsteps had died away, one of them returned, and, after a little hesitation in the passage, knocked at her door.

"Yes?" said Nelly from within.

"It's me—Short," a voice called through the keyhole. "I only wanted to say that we must be off early tomorrow morning, my dear, because unless we get the start of the dogs the villages won't be worth a penny. You'll be sure to be stirring early and go with us? I'll call you."

Nelly answered Yes, and heard him creep away. She felt a little uneasy at the anxiety of these men, especially when she remembered that she had seen them whispering downstairs when she awoke, and that they had looked a little confused. She was too tired to think, however, and soon fell asleep.

Short woke her very early as he had promised, and she started from her bed without delay, and, to the great relief of Short, Nelly and her grandfather were ready as soon as himself.

The morning was fine and warm, and the ground cool to their feet after last night's rain, and the hedges were fresh and green. They had not gone very far when Nelly was again struck by the altered behaviour of Mr Codlin, who, instead of plodding on in his usual sulky style alone, kept close to her, and seemed quite jealous of Short's making himself agreeable as usual with his merry tales and jokes.

She noticed, too, that whenever they parted to give a performance outside a village alehouse, Mr Codlin, while he went through his share of the Punch and Judy play, kept his eye steadily on her, and sometimes was so very obliging that he made the old man lean on his arm, and so held him tight, till they could all move on together again.

Meanwhile, they were drawing near to the town where the races were to begin next day; and people of all descriptions were wending that way. The crowd grew thicker and more noisy, and often a four-horse carriage, dashing by, left them in a cloud of dust.

It was dark before they reached the town itself; and here all was tumult and confusion; the streets were filled with throngs of people, and flags streamed from windows and housetops.

Quickening their steps to get clear of the roar and riot, they at length passed through the town and made for the race-course, which was upon an open heath. Although many people were already there, busily erecting tents, Nelly felt it an escape from the town, and drew her breath more freely.

The purchase of a scanty supper reduced her little stock of money so low that she had only a few halfpence with which to buy a breakfast on the morrow; and now the time had come when they must beg their bread.

They lay down to rest in a corner of a tent and slept soundly in spite of the busy preparations that were going on around them all night; but Nell awoke early, and soon after sunrise next morning she stole out from the tent, and rambling into some fields at a short distance, plucked a few wild roses and such humble flowers, intending to make them into little nosegays and offer them to the ladies in the carriages, when the company arrived.

Her thoughts were not idle while she was thus engaged. Codlin's anxiety to keep her in view still troubled her, and she made up her mind that they must try to steal away from these men at the first opportunity.

She went back to the tent with her flowers, and, sitting by the old man's side, began to tie them up in bunches, while Codlin and Short still lay asleep in another corner.

"Grandfather," said Nell in a low voice, pulling him by the sleeve, "don't look at those I talk about, and don't seem as if I spoke of anything but these flowers. What was that you told me before we left the old house? That if they knew what we were going to do, they would say that you were mad, and part us?"

The old man turned to her with a look of wild terror; but she checked him by a look, and bidding him hold some flowers while she tied them up, and so bringing her lips closer to his ear, said—

"I know that was what you told me. You needn't speak, dear. I recollect it very well. It was not likely that I should forget it. Grandfather, these men suspect that we have secretly left our friends, and mean to carry us before some gentleman, and have us taken care of and sent back. If you let your hand tremble so, we can never get away from them, but if you're only quiet now, we shall do so easily."

"How?" muttered the old man. "Dear Nelly, how? They will shut me up in a stone room, dark and cold, and chain me up to the wall, Nell—flog me with whips, and never let me see thee more."

The old man's illness had left him quite childish; but he had wit enough to be sure that those in authority would think him mad, did they know of his wandering like a beggar about the country, with an inexperienced girl like Nelly for his guide. And his one dread was that he might be separated from the child.

"You're trembling again," said Nelly. "Keep close to me all day. Never mind them; don't look at them, but at me. I shall find a time when we can steal away. When I do, mind you come with me, and do not stop or speak a word. Hush! that's all!"

As the morning wore on, the tents assumed a gayer and a more brilliant appearance, and long lines of carriages came rolling softly on the turf. Black-eyed gipsy-girls, with gaudy handkerchiefs on their heads, sallied forth to tell fortunes. And Jerry, with his dancing dogs, turned up.

Along the uncleared course Short led his party, sounding the brazen trumpet, and revelling in the voice of Punch; and at his heels went Mr Codlin, bearing the show as usual, and keeping his eye on Nelly and her grandfather, as they rather lingered in the rear.

The child bore upon her arm the little basket with her flowers, and sometimes stopped, with timid and modest looks, to offer them at some gay carriage; but although ladies smiled gently as they shook their heads, and others cried to the gentlemen beside them, "See, what a pretty face!" they let the pretty face pass on, and never thought that it looked tired and hungry.

But, after many trampings up and down, one lady called the child towards her, and, taking her flowers, put money into her trembling hand at last.

Many a time they went up and down those long, long lines, seeing everything but the horses and the race. Many a time, too, was Punch displayed, but all this while the eye of Mr Codlin was upon them, and to escape without notice was impossible.

At length, late in the day, Mr Codlin pitched the show in a convenient spot, and the spectators were soon taken up with watching the play. Nelly, with the old man, was sitting on the grass behind it, when some loud laugh at some extra witty joke of Mr Short's roused her from her thoughts and caused her to look behind.

If they were ever to get away unseen, that was the very moment. Short was occupied in working the show, Punch was laying vigorously about him with his cudgel on all sides, the people were looking on with laughing faces, and Mr Codlin had relaxed into a grim smile, as his roving eye spied hands going into waistcoat pockets and groping secretly for six-pences. If they were ever to get away unseen, that was the very moment.

Nelly touched the old man's arm and looked at him. It was enough. They fled. They made a path through booths and carriages, and throngs of people, and never once stopped to look behind. And creeping under the brow of a hill at a quick pace, they made for the open fields.

11

The Schoolmaster

It was not until they were quite exhausted that the old man and the child ventured to stop and sit down to rest upon the borders of a little wood.

But it was some time before she could quiet the trembling old man, who fancied he saw people stealing towards them beneath the cover of the bushes, or lurking in every ditch to seize him and carry him away captive to some gloomy madhouse, where Nell could never come to him, save to look at him through iron bars and gratings in the wall.

His terror was so great that it affected Nelly. Separation from her grandfather was the greatest evil she could dread; and feeling for the time as though, go where they would, they were to be hunted down, and could never be safe but in hiding, the child's heart failed her, and her courage drooped.

But in Nell's delicate frame was enshrined a brave and noble heart; and when she cast her tearful eyes upon the poor old man, and remembered how weak he was, and how helpless he would be if *she* failed him, her heart swelled within her, and she felt strong and brave again.

"We are quite safe now, and have nothing to fear, indeed, dear Grandfather," she said.

"Nothing to fear!" cried the old man. "Nothing to fear if they took me from thee! Nothing to fear if they parted us! Nobody is true to me. No, not one. Not even Nell!"

"Oh! do not say that," replied the child, "for if anybody is true at heart, and earnest, I am. I am sure you know I am."

"Then how," said the old man, looking fearfully round, "how can you bear to think that we are safe, when they are searching for me everywhere, and may come here, and steal upon us, even while we're talking?"

"Because I am sure that we have not been followed," Nelly said. "Judge for yourself, dear Grandfather; look round and see how quiet and still it is. We are alone together, and may ramble where we like. Not safe? Could I feel easy—did I feel easy—when any danger threatened you?"

"True, true," he answered, pressing her hand, but still looking anxiously about. "What noise was that?"

"A bird," said Nelly, "flying into the wood, and leading the way for us to follow. You remember that we said we would walk in woods and fields, and by the side of rivers, and how happy we should be—you remember that? But here, while the sun shines above our heads, and everything is bright and happy, we are sitting sadly down and losing time. See what a pleasant path; and there's the bird—the same bird—now he flies to another tree, and stays to sing. Come!"

And thus she lured the old man on, stopping to listen to the songs that broke the happy silence, or to watch the sun as it trembled through the leaves.

At length the path brought them to the end of the wood, and to a public road. And going along it for a short

distance, they came upon a finger-post pointing up a
narrow lane leading, as it announced, to a village three
miles off, and thither they bent their steps.

It was a very small place. The men and boys were
playing at cricket on the green; and as the other folks
were looking on, they wandered up and down, uncertain
where to seek a humble lodging.

There was but one man in the little garden before his
cottage, and him they were timid of approaching, for he
was the schoolmaster, and had "School" written up over
his window in black letters on a white board.

He was a pale, simple-looking man, slight and spare,
and sat among his flowers and beehives, smoking his
pipe in the little porch before his door.

"Speak to him, dear," the old man whispered.

"I am almost afraid to disturb him," said the child
timidly. "He does not seem to see us. Perhaps if we wait
a little he may look this way."

They waited, but the schoolmaster did not turn to
them, and still sat, thoughtful and silent, in the little
porch. He had a kind face. And as it would soon be dark,
Nelly ventured to draw near, leading her grandfather by
the hand. The slight noise they made in raising the latch
of the wicket-gate caught his attention.

Nell dropped a curtsy, and told him they were poor
travellers who sought a shelter for the night, which they
would gladly pay for, as far as their means allowed. The
schoolmaster looked earnestly at her as she spoke, laid
aside his pipe, and rose up directly.

"If you could direct us anywhere, Sir," said Nell, "we
should take it very kindly.'

"You have been walking a long way?" said the
schoolmaster.

"A long way, Sir," said Nell.

"You're a young traveller, my child," he said, laying his hand gently on her head. "Your grandchild, friend?"

"Ay, Sir," said the old man, "the stay and comfort of my life."

"Come in," said the schoolmaster. And he conducted them, without another word, into his little schoolroom, which was parlour and kitchen as well, and told them they were welcome to remain under his roof till morning.

Before they had done thanking him, he spread a coarse white cloth upon the table, with knives and plates; and bringing out some bread and cold meat and a jug of beer, besought them to eat and drink.

Nell looked round the room as she took her seat. There were a couple of forms, notched and cut and inked all over; a small deal desk perched on four legs, at which no doubt the master sat; and a few dog-eared books upon a shelf. The cane and ruler were displayed on hooks upon the wall, and near them a dunce's cap made of old newspapers. But the great ornaments of the walls were certain texts and proverbs fairly copied in a good round hand.

"Yes," said the poor schoolmaster, seeing that Nell's attention was caught by this. "That's beautiful writing, my dear."

"Very, Sir," replied Nelly; "is it yours?"

"Mine!" said the schoolmaster, taking out his spectacles and putting them on again to look at the beautiful writing. "*I* couldn't write like that nowadays. No. They are all done by one hand; a little hand it is, not so old as yours, but a very clever one." And the schoolmaster stopped and took off his spectacles to wipe them, as though they had grown dim.

"I hope there is nothing the matter, Sir?" said Nelly anxiously.

"Not much, my dear. I hoped to have seen him on the green tonight. He was always foremost among them. But he'll be there tomorrow."

"Has he been ill?" asked Nelly, with a child's quick sympathy.

"Not very. They said he was wandering in his head yesterday, dear boy, and so they said the day before; it's not a bad sign—not at all a bad sign."

Nelly was silent. He walked to the door and looked wistfully out. The shadows of the night were gathering, and all was still.

By-and-by he lighted a candle, fastened the window shutter, and closed the door. But after he had sat silent for a little time he took down his hat, and said he would go and see how his little pupil was, if Nell would sit up till he returned.

Nell was quite willing, and after he was gone she persuaded her grandfather to go to bed in the little room the schoolmaster had shown to her; she felt the place very lonely and strange, but the schoolmaster returned in half-an-hour's time, and took his seat silently in the chimney corner. Then he turned to her, and, speaking very gently, said he hoped she would say a prayer that night for a sick child.

"My favourite scholar!" said the poor schoolmaster, looking mournfully round the walls. "It is a little hand to have done all that, and to waste away with sickness. It is a very, very little hand."

12

His Favourite Scholar

Nell slept soundly in a chamber under the thatched roof, and, rising early, descended to the room where she had supped last night. As the schoolmaster had already left his bed and gone out to inquire how the boy was, Nell bestirred herself to make it neat and comfortable, and had just finished her work when her kind host returned.

He thanked her many times, and said that the dame who usually did such offices for him had gone to nurse the little scholar. Nell asked if he were better.

"No," said the poor schoolmaster, shaking his head sorrowfully, "no better. They even say he is worse."

"I am very sorry for that, Sir," said Nell.

The poor schoolmaster looked pleased at her sympathy; but added in his quiet, patient way, "I hope it is not so. I don't think he can be worse."

Nell asked him to let her prepare the breakfast, and, her grandfather coming down a little later, the three partook of it together.

"If the journey you have before you is a long one," said the kind host, seeing that the old man seemed much fatigued, "you're very welcome to pass another night here. I should really be glad if you would, friend."

"What are we to do, Nell?" said the old man helplessly. "Say what we are to do, dear."

Nelly was only too thankful to stay and rest in that peaceful spot; and to show her gratitude to the kind schoolmaster, busied herself in such household duties as she could perform for him, and then, taking some needlework from her basket, sat down upon a stool beside the lattice, where the honeysuckle and woodbine entwined their tender stems. Her grandfather was basking in the sun outside, breathing the perfume of flowers; and the schoolmaster, after arranging the two forms in due order, took his seat behind the desk and waited for his scholars.

Nell, afraid that she might be in the way, offered to withdraw to her little bedroom. But this he would not allow, and as he seemed pleased to have her there, she remained, and went on with her sewing.

"Have you many scholars, Sir?" she asked.

The poor schoolmaster shook his head, and said that they barely filled the two forms.

"Are the others clever, Sir?" asked Nell, glancing at the beautiful writing on the wall.

"Good boys," said the schoolmaster, "good boys enough, my dear, but they'll never do like that."

As he spoke a little flaxen-haired boy came in, and then another, and so on till the forms were occupied by a dozen boys or so.

At the top of the first form—the post of honour in the school—was the vacant place of the little sick scholar. No boy attempted to take it; it was left empty; and some of the boys looked from it to the schoolmaster, and whispered behind their hands.

Then began the hum of conning over lessons and getting them by heart, and in the midst of the din sat the poor schoolmaster trying to fix his mind upon the duties of the day, and to forget his favourite scholar.

"I think, boys," said the schoolmaster when the clock struck twelve, "that I shall give an extra half-holiday this afternoon."

At this the boys gave a lusty shout, but the schoolmaster held up his hand for them to be silent.

"You must promise me first," said the schoolmaster, "that you'll not be noisy. Be as happy as you can, and don't be unmindful that you are blessed with health. Goodbye all."

"Thank'ee, Sir," and, "Goodbye, Sir," were said a great many times, and the boys went out very slowly and softly.

Towards night an old woman came tottering up the garden, and meeting the schoolmaster at the door, said he was to go to Dame West's directly. He was just going to take Nell for a little walk, and without letting go her hand the schoolmaster hurried away.

They stopped at a cottage door, and the school-master knocked softly at it with his hand. It was opened without loss of time, and he followed the woman who had summoned him into another room, where his little friend lay stretched upon a bed.

He was a very young boy, quite a little child. His hair still hung in curls about his face, and his eyes were very bright; but their light was of Heaven, not of earth. The schoolmaster took a seat beside him, and, stooping over the pillow, whispered his name. The boy sprang up, stroked his face with his hand, and threw his wasted arms around his neck, crying out that he was his dear, kind friend.

"I hope I always was. I meant to be, God knows," said the poor schoolmaster.

"Who is that?" said the boy, seeing Nell. "I am afraid to kiss her, lest I should make her ill. Ask her to shake hands with me."

Nell came closer with the tears rolling down her face, and took his little languid hand in hers.

"You remember the garden, Harry," whispered the schoolmaster, anxious to rouse him, for a dullness seemed gathering upon the child, "and how pleasant it used to be in the evening time?"

The boy smiled faintly—so very, very faintly—and put his hand upon his friend's grey head. He moved his lips, too, but no voice came from them; no, not a sound.

In the silence that followed, the hum of distant voices borne upon the evening air came floating through the open window.

"What's that?" said the sick child, opening his eyes.

"The boys at play upon the green."

He took a handkerchief from his pillow, and tried to wave it above his head. But the feeble arm dropped powerless down.

"Shall I do it?" said the schoolmaster.

"Please wave it at the window," was the faint reply. "Tie it to the lattice. Some of them may see it there. Perhaps they will think of me, and look this way."

He raised his head and glanced from the fluttering handkerchief to his idle bat, that lay with slate and book, and other boyish property, upon a table in the room. And then he laid him softly down again, and asked if the little girl were there, for he could not see her.

Nell stepped forward, and pressed the passive hand that lay on the coverlet. The two old friends and companions—for such they were, though they were man and child—held each other in a long embrace, and then the little scholar turned his face towards the wall, and fell asleep.

The poor schoolmaster sat in the same place, holding the small, cold hand in his, and chafing it. It was but the hand of a dead child. He felt that, and yet he chafed still, and could not lay it down.

Almost broken-hearted, Nell withdrew with the schoolmaster from the bedside and returned to the cottage.

That night her dreams were of the little scholar; not in a coffin and covered up, but mingling with angels, and smiling happily. The sun darting his cheerful rays into the room awoke her; and now they must take leave of the poor schoolmaster, and wander forth again.

They had their breakfast, and by the time they were ready to depart, school had begun. The schoolmaster rose from his desk, and walked with them to the gate.

With a trembling and reluctant hand Nell held out to him the money which the lady had given her at the races for her flowers, faltering in her thanks as she thought how small the sum was, and blushing as she offered it. But he bade her keep it, and stooped to kiss her cheek.

"Good fortune and happiness go with you!" said the poor schoolmaster. "I am quite a solitary man now. If you ever pass this way again, you'll not forget the little village school."

"We shall never forget it, Sir," rejoined Nelly, "nor ever forget to be grateful to you for your kindness to us."

They bade him farewell very many times, and turned away, resolving to keep to the main road, and go wherever it might lead them.

13

The Lady of the Caravan

It was a long, long road, and very lonely. Occasionally they passed a cluster of cottages; and later in the day they came to a roadside public-house, where they bought some bread and cheese.

On, on, over the dull, winding road, which seemed to be leading to nothing. They were very tired, but they were obliged to go on to find some place of shelter for the night.

The afternoon had worn away into a beautiful evening, when they arrived at a point where the road made a sharp turn, and struck across a common. On the border of this common, and close to the hedge which divided it from the cultivated fields, a caravan was drawn up to rest.

It was not a shabby, dingy, dusty cart, but a smart little house upon wheels, with white curtains in the windows, and shutters which were brightly painted red and green. Neither was it a poor caravan drawn by a single donkey or half-starved horse, for a pair of fat horses were grazing near by on the frouzy grass. Neither was it a gipsy caravan, for at the open door sat a Christian lady, stout and comfortable to look upon, who wore a large bonnet trembling with bows; and she was having her tea.

The tea-things, which included a cold knuckle of ham, were set forth upon a drum, covered with a white napkin, and at this convenient round table sat this roving lady, drinking her tea out of a breakfast cup.

She had just put the cup down when she spied an old man and a young girl walking slowly by, and glancing at her proceedings with eyes of modest but hungry admiration.

"Hey!" cried the lady of the caravan, scooping the crumbs out of her lap and swallowing the same before wiping her lips. "Yes, to be sure—who won the Helter-Skelter Plate, child?"

"Won what, Ma'am?" asked Nell.

"The Helter-Skelter Plate at the races, child—the Plate that was run for on the second day?"

"I don't know, Ma'am."

"Don't know! Why, you were there. I saw you with my own eyes."

Nell was not a little alarmed to hear this, supposing that the lady might be intimately acquainted with Short and Codlin; but her next words reassured her.

"And very sorry I was," said the lady of the caravan, "to see you in company with a Punch; a low, practical, vulgar wretch, that people should scorn to look at."

"I was not there by choice," returned Nell; "we didn't know our way, and the two men were very kind to us, and let us travel with them. Do you—do you know them, Ma'am?"

"Know 'em, child!" cried the lady of the caravan in a sort of shriek. "Know *them!* Do I look as if I knowed 'em; does the caravan look as if *it* knowed 'em?"

"No, no, Ma'am, no," said Nell, fearing she had committed some fault. "I beg your pardon."

It was granted immediately. And Nell explained that

they had left the races on the first day; and ventured to
inquire how far the next town was, as they purposed to
spend the night there, and was greatly discouraged to
learn that it was eight miles off.

The grandfather sighed wearily, but he made no
complaint, and Nell could hardly keep back her tears as
she glanced at the darkening road. The child thanked her
for the information, and giving her hand to the old man
was leading him away, when the lady of the caravan,
who was beginning to clear her table, noticed the child's
anxious manner; she hesitated and stopped, and called
Nell to return.

"Come nearer, nearer still," said she, beckoning her to
go up the steps of the caravan. "Are you hungry, child?"

"Not very, but we are tired, and it's—it *is* a long way—"

"Well, hungry or not, you'd better have some tea,"
rejoined her new acquaintance. "I suppose you're
agreeable to that, old gentleman?"

The grandfather humbly pulled off his hat and thanked
her. The lady of the caravan then bade him come up the
steps likewise; but the drum was not a convenient table
for two, so they went down the steps again and sat upon
the grass, where she handed down to them the tea-tray,
the bread and butter, and the knuckle of ham.

"Set 'em out near the hind wheels, child; that's the best
place," said their new friend. "Now hand up the teapot
for a little more hot water, and a pinch of fresh tea, and
then both of you eat and drink as much as you can, and
don't spare anything; that's all I ask of you."

The travellers made a hearty meal, and, needless to
say, enjoyed it to the utmost.

While they were thus engaged, the lady of the caravan
came down the steps, and with her hands clasped behind
her, and her large bonnet trembling very much, walked

up and down in a very stately manner. By-and-by she sat down upon the steps and called, "George!" whereupon a man in a carter's frock, who had been nearly hidden in a hedge, appeared in a sitting posture, supporting on his knees a baking-dish and a half-gallon stone-bottle, and bearing in his right hand a knife, and in his left a fork.

"Yes, Missus" said George.

"How did you find the cold pie, George?"

"It warn't amiss, Mum."

"We are not a heavy load, George?"

"That's always what the ladies say," replied the man. "If cattle have got their proper load, you never can persuade a woman that they'll not bear something more. What is the cause of this here?"

"Would these two travellers make much difference to the horses if we took them with us?" asked his Mistress, pointing to Nell and the old man. "They can't be very heavy."

"The weight o' the pair, Mum," said George, eyeing them carefully, "would be a trifle under that of Oliver Cromwell."

Nell was much surprised that the man should be so accurately acquainted with the weight of one who had lived so long before their time; but speedily forgot the subject in the joy of hearing that they were to go forward in the caravan, for which she thanked the lady very earnestly.

She helped to put away the tea-things, and other matters that were lying about, with great readiness; and the horses being by that time harnessed, Nell got into the caravan, followed by her delighted grandfather.

The mistress then shut the door and sat herself down by her drum at an open window; the steps were stowed by George under the carriage, and away they went with a great creaking and straining, jolting heavily along.

One half of the caravan—the half in which the comfortable proprietress was then seated—was carpeted, and so partitioned off at the further end as to form a sleeping place like a berth on board ship. The other half served for a kitchen, and was fitted up with a stove whose small chimney passed through the roof. It held also a larder, several chests, a great pitcher of water, some pots and pans, and articles of crockery.

The two travellers spoke in whispers, until the old man fell asleep, and then the lady of the caravan invited Nell to come and sit beside her.

"Well, child," she said, "how do you like this way of travelling?"

Nell said that she thought it very pleasant indeed; and after a while the mistress got up and brought out of a corner a roll of canvas about a yard wide, which she laid upon the floor and spread open with her foot until it nearly reached from one end of the caravan to the other.

"There, child," she said, "read that."

Nell walked down it, and read aloud, in enormous black letters:

"JARLEY'S WAX-WORK."

"That's me," said the lady. "I am Mrs Jarley."

Then she unfolded other scrolls on which were written inscriptions such as:

"ONE HUNDRED FIGURES THE FULL SIZE OF LIFE";
"JARLEY IS THE DELIGHT OF THE NOBILITY AND GENTRY";
"THE ROYAL FAMILY ARE THE PATRONS OF JARLEY."

On another scroll Nell read a piece of poetry beginning:

> "If I knowed a donkey wot wouldn't go
> To see Mrs Jarley's Wax-Work Show,
> Do you think I'd acknowledge him?
> Oh no no!
>   Then run to Jarley's—"

When Nell had read them all, Mrs Jarley rolled them up, and, having put them carefully away, sat down again, and looked at the child in triumph.

"Never go into the company of a filthy Punch any more," said Mrs Jarley, "after this."

"I never saw any wax-work, Ma'am," said Nell. "Is it funnier than Punch?"

"Funnier!" said Mrs Jarley in a shrill voice. "It is not funny at all!"

"Is it here, Ma'am?" asked Nell.

"Is what here, child?"

"The wax-work, Ma'am."

"Why, bless you, child, what are you thinking of? How could such a collection be here, when you see everything except the inside of one little cupboard and a few boxes? It's gone on in the other wans to the Assembly-rooms, and there it'll be exhibited the day after tomorrow. You are going to the same town and you'll see it, I dare say."

"I shall not be in the town, I think, Ma'am," said Nell.

"Not there!" cried Mrs Jarley. "Then where will you be?"

"I—I—don't quite know. I am not certain."

"You don't mean to say that you're travelling about the

country without knowing where you're going to?" said Mrs Jarley. "What curious people you are! You looked to me at the races, child, as if you had got there by accident."

"We were there quite by accident," said Nell, confused by this questioning. "We are poor people, Ma'am, and we are only wandering about. We have nothing to do;—I only wish we had."

"You amaze me more and more," said Mrs Jarley. "Why, what do you call yourselves? Not beggars?"

"Indeed, Ma'am, I don't know what else we are," returned the child.

"Bless me!" said the lady of the caravan, "I never heard of such a thing. Who'd have thought it?"

She remained long silent in her surprise. "And yet you can read," she went on, "and write too, I shouldn't wonder?"

"Yes, Ma'am," said Nell.

"Well, and what a thing that is," returned Mrs Jarley. "I can't!" She fell into a thoughtful silence; for, truth to tell, she was much taken by Nell's refinement, and the beauty of her face, and seemed suddenly struck by an idea which she was turning over in her mind.

At length she summoned the driver to come under the window at which she was seated, and while Nell withdrew and joined her grandfather who was now awake, Mrs Jarley held a long conversation with George, as if she were asking his advice upon some important point.

Then she drew in her head again, and beckoned Nell to approach.

"And the old gentleman, too," said Mrs Jarley, "for I want to have a word with him. Do you want a good situation for your granddaughter, Master? If you do, I can put her in the way of getting one. What do you say?"

"I can't leave her," answered the old man. "We can't separate. What would become of me without her?"

"I should have thought you were old enough to take care of yourself," said Mrs Jarley sharply.

"But he never will be," put in the child in an earnest whisper. "I fear he never will be again. Pray do not speak harshly to him. We are very thankful to you," she added aloud, "but neither of us could part from the other if all the wealth in the world were halved between us."

Mrs Jarley seemed disappointed, and looked at the old man, who tenderly took Nell's hand, as if she could very well have dispensed with his company. After an awkward pause she thrust her head out of the window again, and had another consultation with the driver which lasted a long time. Then she drew her head in again, and addressed the grandfather.

"If you're really disposed to employ yourself," said Mrs Jarley, "there would be plenty for you to do in helping to dust the figures, and take the checks, and so forth. What I want your granddaughter for is to point 'em to the company; they would soon be learnt, and she has a way with her that people wouldn't think unpleasant. It isn't a common offer, bear in mind. It's Jarley's Wax-Work, remember. The duty's very light and genteel, and the company particular select." She went on to add that she could not offer any certain salary until she had seen what Nell could do, but board and lodging, both for her and her grandfather, she bound herself to provide.

Nell and her grandfather consulted together, while Mrs Jarley walked up and down majestically in the caravan. "Now, child," she cried, coming to a halt as Nell turned towards her.

"We are very much obliged to you, Ma'am," said Nell, "and thankfully accept your offer."

"And you'll never be sorry for it," said Mrs Jarley; "I'm pretty sure of that. So as that's all settled, let us have a bit of supper."

14

Mrs Jarley's Waxwork Show

In the meanwhile the caravan jolted on, and came at last upon the paved streets of a town which were clear of passengers, and quiet; for it was by this time near midnight, and the townspeople were all in bed. It being too late to repair to the Exhibition-room, they turned aside into a piece of waste ground that lay just within the old town-gate, and drew up there for the night, near to another caravan which also bore the great name of Jarley on its panel.

This caravan was empty, as the wax-work figures had been taken out of it to the Exhibition-room; so Mrs Jarley suggested that it would make a nice room for the old man, and in it Nelly made him up the best bed she could from the materials with which Mrs Jarley supplied her. Nell, herself, was to sleep in Mrs Jarley's own travelling-carriage, as a mark of that great lady's favour.

Her bed was already made up upon the floor, and she fell into a deep, calm sleep, and never opened her eyes till late next morning—so late that she found Mrs Jarley up and dressed and actively engaged in preparing breakfast.

Nell apologised for being so late, but Mrs Jarley said

good-humouredly that she would not have roused her if she had slept till noon.

"Because it does you good," said the lady of the caravan, "when you're tired to sleep as long as ever you can, and get the fatigue quite off."

Breakfast was soon ready, and so was the old man, and the three sat down together. The meal finished, Nell assisted to wash up the cups and saucers, and put them in their proper places; and then Mrs Jarley arrayed herself in an exceedingly bright shawl for the purpose of walking through the streets of the town.

"The wan will come to bring the boxes," said Mrs Jarley, "and you had better come in it, child. I am obliged to walk, very much against my will; but the people expect it of me, and public characters can't be their own masters and mistresses in such matters as these. How do I look, child?"

Nell returned a satisfactory reply, and Mrs Jarvey went forth majestically. At last the caravan stopped at the place of exhibition. The chests were carried out of the caravan, and taken in to be unlocked by Mrs Jarley, who, attended by George and another man in velveteen knickerbockers and a drab hat, were waiting to decorate the room with the festoons and other ornaments that the chests contained.

They all got to work without loss of time, and both Nell and the old man were of great service in helping to ornament the place. When the festoons were all put up as tastily as might be, the wax figures were uncovered, for they had been concealed with cloths up to this, to keep the dust from injuring their complexions; and they were displayed on a platform, where they stood in glittering dresses of all times and climes, with their eyes very wide open, and their countenances expressing great surprise.

When Nell had exhausted her first raptures at this glorious sight, Mrs Jarley ordered the room to be cleared of all but herself and the child, and sitting down in an armchair in the centre, put a willow wand—long used by herself for pointing out the characters—into Nell's hand, and took great pains to instruct her in her duty.

"That," said Mrs Jarley in her exhibition tone, as Nell touched a figure at the beginning of the platform, "is an unfortunate Maid of Honour in the time of Queen Elizabeth, who died from pricking her finger in consequence of working on a Sunday. Observe the blood which is trickling from her finger; also the gold-eyed needle of the period, with which she is at work."

All this Nell repeated two or three times, pointing to the finger and the needle at the right times, and then passed on to the next.

"That, ladies and gentlemen," said Mrs Jarley, "is Jasper Packlemerton of atrocious memory, who courted and married fourteen wives, and destroyed them all by tickling the soles of their feet. Observe that his fingers are curled in the act of tickling, and that his face is represented with a wink, as he appeared when committing his barbarous murders."

When Nell knew all about Mr Packlemerton, and could say it without faltering, Mrs Jarley passed on to the fat man, then to the thin man, the old lady who died of dancing at a hundred-and-thirty-two, the wild boy of the woods, the woman who poisoned thirty families with pickled walnuts, and many other notorious characters.

Nell had such a good memory that in two hours' time she had the history of every figure by heart, and Mrs Jarley was highly delighted with her quickness and cleverness, and was not slow to tell her so.

Another of Nell's duties was to go round the town

decorated with artificial flowers in a light cart, dispensing handbills to the people in the street, accompanied by two men, one beating a drum, the other blowing a trumpet.

The child's beauty caused quite a sensation in the little town, till at last, Mrs Jarley, fearing that Nell should become too cheap, kept her in the Exhibition-room, where she described the figures to admiring audiences.

Nell found in Mrs Jarley a very kind and considerate mistress, who not only liked to be comfortable herself, but insisted on having those about her comfortable too. Many were the odd sixpences and threepenny bits that found their way into Nell's hands from the admiring visitors, which Nell was allowed to put into her own purse, her kind mistress never demanding any toll. And as her grandfather was well treated and useful himself, she felt that they had fallen on pleasant times.

15

At the Lone Inn

One evening, a holiday night with them, Nell and her father went out for a walk. They got out of the town, and took a footpath which struck through some pleasant fields, and were tempted to walk on till they found themselves further off than they had at first intended to go.

They sat down to rest before turning back, and did not notice that it was gradually getting overcast; and now the sky had become dark and lowering. They were returning along the high-road when large drops of rain began to fall; then the low rumbling of thunder was heard, and the lightning flashed.

Afraid of taking shelter under a tree or hedge, they hurried along, hoping to find some house where they could seek a refuge from the storm which had now burst forth in earnest.

Drenched with pelting rain, and confused by the deafening thunder, they came at last on a solitary house, where a man standing at the door shouted to them to come in.

"You'd better stand by the fire here, and dry yourselves a bit," he said. "This is a public-house. *The Valiant Soldier*

is pretty well known hereabouts." He also informed
them that his name was Jem Groves.

It was a warm summer night and there was a large
screen across the room to keep the fire off, and they
could hear that some people were on the other side of the
screen; and presently a gruff voice bade Mr Groves
"hold his noise and light a candle."

Suddenly the old grandfather grew interested. "Nell,
they're—they're playing cards," he whispered. "Don't
you hear them?"

"Look sharp with that candle," said the voice—
"Game! Seven and sixpence to me, old Isaac. Hand over!"

"Do you hear, Nell, do you hear them?" whispered the
old man with increased earnestness, as the money
clinked upon the table.

And then the voice behind the screen said, "Old
Luke's winning through thick and thin of late years,
though I remember the time when he was the unluckiest
and unfortunest of men."

"Do you hear what he says?" whispered the old man.
"Do you hear that, Nell?"

The child saw with astonishment and alarm that his
whole appearance had undergone a complete change.
His face was flushed and eager, and the hand he laid
upon her arm trembled so violently that she shook
beneath its grasp.

"Bear witness," he muttered, looking upward, "that I
always said it; that I knew it, dreamed it, felt it was the
truth, and that it must be so! What money have we, Nell?
Come! I saw you with money yesterday. What money
have we? Give it to me."

"No, no, let me keep it, Grandfather!" said the
frightened child. "Let us go away from here. Do not
mind the rain. Pray let us go."

"Give it to me, I say!" returned the old man fiercely. "Hush, hush, don't cry, Nell. If I spoke sharply, dear, I didn't mean it. It's for thy good. I have wronged thee, Nell, but I will right thee yet. I will indeed. Where is the money?"

"Do not take it," said the child. "Pray do not take it, dear. For both our sakes let me keep it, or let me throw it away—better let me throw it away than that you should take it now. Let us go, do let us go."

"Give me the money," repeated the old man. "I must have it. There—there—that's my dear Nell. I'll right thee one day, child. I'll right thee, never fear!"

She took from her pocket her little purse. He seized it as impatiently as he had spoken, and hastily made his way to the other side of the screen. It was impossible to restrain him, and the trembling child followed close behind.

There were two men behind the screen who had a pack of cards and some silver money between them, while upon the screen itself the games they had played were scored in chalk.

One of the men, called Isaac, looked round and asked the old man what he wanted, and suggested that perhaps he wished to take a hand with them.

"That's what I mean," cried the excited old man, shaking Nell's purse in his eager hand; and then throwing it down upon the table he gathered up the cards as a miser would clutch at gold.

"We'll make a four-handed game of it, and take in Groves," said the other man. "Come, Jemmy."

The landlord, like one well used to such little parties, approached the table and took his seat.

The child, in a perfect agony, drew her grandfather aside, and implored him, even then, to come away.

"Come, and we may be so happy," said Nell.

"We *will* be happy," said the old man hastily. "Let me go, Nell. I shall but win back my own, and it's all for thee, my darling."

"God help us!" cried the child. "Oh! what hard fortune brought us here?"

The old man took his seat, and the frightened child sat near, watching him so wild and restless as the game went on, so feverishly anxious, so terribly eager, so ravenous for the paltry stakes, that she could almost have better borne to see him dead.

The storm had raged for full three hours, and still the game went on, and still the anxious child was forgotten. At length the play came to an end; the man Isaac rose the only winner; and Nell's little purse lay empty on the table.

"Patience, patience, and we'll right thee yet," whispered the old man. "Lose today, win tomorrow. Come. I'm ready."

"Do you know what the time is?" said Mr Groves, who was smoking with his friends. "Past twelve o'clock!"

"It's very late," said the uneasy child. "I wish we had gone before. What will they think of us? It will be two o'clock by the time we get back. What would it cost, Sir, if we stopped here?"

"Two good beds, one-and-sixpence; supper and beer, one shilling; total, two shillings and sixpence."

Now Nell had still the piece of gold sewn in her dress; and when she came to consider the lateness of the hour, and the consternation in which they would throw Mrs Jarley by knocking her up in the middle of the night, she took her grandfather aside, and telling him she had enough to pay for a night's lodging, proposed that they should stay there for the night.

"If I had had but that money before—if I had only known of it a few minutes ago!" muttered the old man.

"We will decide to stop here, if you please," said Nell, turning hastily to the landlord.

"I think that's prudent," said Mr Groves. "You shall have your suppers directly."

As they were to leave the house very early in the morning, Nell was anxious to pay for their lodgings before they retired to bed. But she felt she must conceal her little hoard from her grandfather; and having taken the piece of gold from her dress secretly, she watched her opportunity and followed the landlord when he went out of the room, and asked him to change it for her in the little bar.

"Will you give me the change here, if you please?" said Nell.

Mr Groves was surprised. But thinking that it was no business of his, he counted out the change, and gave it to her. Nell was returning to the room where they had passed the evening, when she fancied she saw a figure just gliding in at the door. And the thought struck her that she had been watched. But by whom?

When she re-entered the room she found its inmates exactly as she had left them. And there was nobody else at the inn. By-and-by she asked her grandfather, in a whisper, whether anybody had left the room while she was absent.

"No," he said, "nobody."

It must have been her fancy, then; and while she was thinking of it a girl came to light her to bed.

The old man took leave of the company at the same time, and they went upstairs together. It was a great, rambling house, with dull passages and wide staircases. She left her grandfather in his chamber, and followed her guide to another, which was at the end of a passage, up some half a dozen steps.

The child did not feel comfortable when she was left alone. She could not help thinking of the figure stealing through the passage downstairs. The men were very ill-looking. They might get their living by robbing travellers. Who could tell?

But putting aside these fancied terrors, Nell thought of the real trouble that had befallen them. Here was the old passion for gambling awakened again in her grandfather's breast, and to what it might lead them Heaven only knew.

And what did Mrs Jarley think of their absence? Would she forgive them in the morning? Or would they be turned adrift again? Oh, why had they stopped in that strange place! It would have been better—far better—to have gone on in the rain.

At last sleep gradually stole upon her, from which she awoke; and then— What! That figure in the room!

A figure was there. Yes, she had drawn up the blind to admit the light when it should dawn, and there, between the foot of the bed and the window, it crouched and slunk along, groping its way with noiseless hands, and stealing round the bed. She had no voice to cry for help, no power to move, but lay still watching it.

On it came—on, silently and stealthily to the bed's head—the breath so near her pillow that she shrank back into it, lest those wandering hands should light upon her face. Back again it stole to the window; and still keeping the face towards her, it busied its hands in something, and she heard the chink of money.

Then on it came again, silently and stealthily as before, and, replacing the garments it had taken from the bedside, dropped upon its hands and knees and crawled away. It reached the door at last, and stood upon its feet. The steps creaked beneath its noiseless tread, and it was gone!

The first impulse of the child was to fly from the terror of being by herself in that room—to have somebody by—not to be alone. Hardly knowing what she did, Nell sprang up and ran to the door.

There was the dreadful shadow pausing at the bottom of the steps. She could not pass it; she might have done so in the darkness, without being seized, but her blood curdled at the thought.

The figure moved again. The child involuntarily did the same. Once in her grandfather's room she would be safe.

It crept along the passage until it came to the very door she longed so ardently to reach, and the figure stopped again.

The idea flashed suddenly upon her—what if it entered there, and had a design upon the old man's life! She turned faint and sick. It did! It went in! There was a light inside. The figure was now within the chamber, and she, still dumb—quite dumb, and almost senseless—stood looking on.

The door was partly open. Not knowing what she meant to do, but meaning to preserve him or be killed herself, she staggered forward and looked in. What sight was that which met her view!

The bed had not been lain in, but was smooth and empty. And at the table sat the old man himself; the only living creature there; his white face pinched and sharpened by the greediness which made his eyes unnaturally bright, counting the money of which his hands had robbed her.

16

Nell Pleads with Him

With faltering steps the child withdrew from the door, and groped her way back to her own room. The terror she had lately felt was nothing compared with that which now oppressed her. No strange robber, stealing to their beds to kill them in their sleep, could have awakened in her bosom half the dread which the recognition of her silent visitor inspired.

The grey-headed old man, gliding like a ghost into her room, and acting the thief while he supposed her fast asleep, then bearing off his prize, and hanging over it with the ghastly exultation she had witnessed, was worse—oh, worse, and far more dreadful, than anything her wildest fancy could have suggested.

If he should return—there was no lock or bolt upon the door—and if, thinking he had left some money yet behind, he should come back to seek for more—

She could hardly connect her own affectionate companion with this old man; so like, yet so unlike him. She had wept to see him dull and quiet. How much greater cause had she for weeping now!

The child sat watching and thinking of these things so long that she felt it would be a relief to hear the old man's voice, or, if he was asleep, even to see him and banish some of the fears that clustered round his image.

She stole down the stairs and passage again. The door was still ajar, as she had left it, and the candle burning as before.

She had her own candle in her hand, prepared to say, if he were waking, that she was uneasy and could not rest, and had come to see if his was still alight. Looking into the room, she saw him lying calmly on his bed, and so took courage to enter.

Fast asleep—no passion in the face, no avarice, no anxiety, no wild desire—all gentle, tranquil and at peace. *This* was not the gambler, or the shadow in her room; this was the dear old friend, her harmless fellow-traveller, her good, kind grandfather.

She had no fear as she looked upon his sleeping face, but she had a deep and weighty sorrow, and it found relief in tears.

"God bless him!" said the child, stooping softly to kiss his placid cheek. "I see too well now that they would indeed part us if they found us out, and shut him up from the light of the sun and sky. He has only me to help him. God bless us both!"

Lighting her candle, she retreated as silently as she had come, and, gaining her room once more, sat up during the remainder of that long, long, miserable night.

The day broke at last and she fell asleep, but was soon roused by the girl who had promised to wake her early; and as soon as she was dressed, prepared to go down to her grandfather. But first she searched her pocket and found that her money was all gone—not a sixpence remained.

The old man was ready, and they were soon on their road. She thought he rather avoided her eye, and appeared to expect that she would tell him of her loss. She felt she must do that or he might suspect the truth.

"Grandfather," she said in a tremulous voice, after they had walked about a mile in silence, "do you think they are honest people at the house yonder?"

"Why?" returned the old man trembling. "Do I think them honest—yes, they played honestly."

"I'll tell you why I ask," said Nell. "I lost some money last night—out of my bedroom I am sure. Unless it was taken by somebody in jest—only in jest, dear Grandfather, which would make me laugh heartily if I could but know it—"

"Who would take money in jest?" returned the old man hurriedly. "Those who take money, take it to keep. Don't talk of jest."

"Then it was stolen out of my room, dear," said Nell, whose last hope was destroyed by the manner of his reply.

"But is there no more, Nell? No more anywhere? Was it all taken—every farthing of it—was there nothing left?"

"Nothing," replied the child.

"We must get more," said the old man, "we must earn it, Nell; hoard it up, scrape it together, come by it somehow. Never mind this loss. Tell nobody of it, and perhaps we may regain it. Don't ask how;—but tell nobody, or trouble may come of it. And so they took it out of thy room when thou wert asleep!" he added in a compassionate tone, very different from the secret, cunning way in which he had spoken until now. "Poor Nell, poor little Nell!"

The child hung down her head and wept. The sympathising tone in which he spoke was quite sincere; she was sure of that.

"All the losses that ever were are not worth tears from thy eyes, darling," said he. "Why should they be, when we will win them back?"

"Let them go," said Nell, looking up. "Let them go once and for ever; and I would never shed another tear if every penny had been a thousand pounds."

"Well, well," said the old man, "she knows no better. I ought to be thankful for it."

"But listen to me," said Nell earnestly. "Will you listen to me?"

"Ay, ay, I'll listen," returned the old man; but he would not look at her; "a pretty voice. It has always a sweet sound to me. It always had when it was her mother's, poor child."

"Let me persuade you, then—oh, do let me persuade you to think no more of gains or losses, and to try no fortune but the fortune we pursue together. Have we been worse off," said Nell, "since we forgot these cares, and have been travelling together? Have we not been much better and happier without a home to shelter us, than ever we were in that unhappy house when these cares were on your mind?"

"She speaks the truth," murmured the old man in the same tone as before. "It must not turn me, but it is the truth—no doubt it is."

"Only remember what we have been since that bright morning when we turned our backs upon it for the last time," said Nell; "only remember what we have been since we have been free of all those miseries—what peaceful days and quiet nights we have had—what happiness we have enjoyed."

He stopped her with a motion of his hand, and bade her talk to him no more just then, for he was busy. By-and-by he kissed her cheek, but would not let her speak.

When they got home, they found Mrs Jarley still in bed. She had sat up for them till past eleven o'clock, and had been uneasy on their account; but guessing that they had been overtaken by the storm and had sought shelter for the night, she went to bed feeling they would not return before morning. And in her usual comfortable way she never dreamed of reproaching them.

That evening, as Nell had dreaded, her grandfather stole away, and did not come back till the night was far spent. Worn out as she was, tired in mind and body, she sat up alone, counting the minutes until he returned—penniless, broken-spirited, wretched; but still bent on his infatuation.

"Get me money," he said wildly, as they parted for the night. "I must have money, Nell. It shall be paid thee back with gallant interest one day; but all the money that comes into thy hands must be mine—not for myself, but to use for thee. Remember, Nell, to use for thee."

What could the child do but give him every penny that came into her hands, lest, in his madness, he should be tempted to rob their benefactress? If she told the truth (so the child thought), he would be treated as a madman; if she did not supply him with money, he would supply himself.

Distracted by these thoughts; borne down by the weight of the sorrow which she dare not tell even to kind Mrs Jarley; the colour forsook Nell's cheek, her eye grew dim, and her heart was oppressed and heavy. The old sorrows she had known in the old, gloomy house had come back again, and haunted her in her dreams.

17

Nell Saves Him from Crime

Between the old man and herself there had come a gradual separation, harder to bear than any former sorrow. Every evening, and often in the daytime too, he was absent, alone; and although she well knew where he went, and why—too well from the constant drain upon the scanty purse and from his haggard looks—he avoided all inquiry, kept a strict reserve, and even shunned her presence.

One evening she was pondering sadly upon this change; for now she took her rambles all alone; when the distant church clock struck nine. Rising at the sound, Nell turned towards the town.

She had gained a little wooden bridge, which, thrown across the stream, led into a meadow in her way, when she came suddenly upon a ruddy light, and, looking forward more attentively, saw that it proceeded from what appeared to be an encampment of gypsies, who had made a fire in one corner at no great distance from the path, and were sitting or lying round it. Nell quickened her pace a little, but kept straight on.

When she approached the spot, she glanced with timid

curiosity toward the fire. Whose was that form between the fire and herself that caused her to stop abruptly?

No, no, it could not be; she was mistaken, she was sure; and on she went again. But at that instant the tones of a voice that spoke—she could not distinguish words—fell familiarly on her ear.

She turned, and looked back. The person had been seated before, but was now in a standing posture, and leaning forward upon a stick on which he rested both his hands. It *was* her grandfather.

Nell's first impulse was to call to him; the next to wonder who his associates could be, and for what purpose they were there together.

With a vague fear Nell drew nearer to the place, not across the open field, however, but creeping towards it by the hedge. In this way she advanced within a few feet of the fire, and, standing among a few young trees, could both see and hear without much danger of being observed.

There were three men, and her grandfather was one of them; the others she recognised as the card-players she had seen at the public-house on the eventful night of the storm—the man whom they had called Isaac and his gruff companion.

"Well, are you going?" said the gruff man, looking into her grandfather's face. "You were in a mighty hurry a minute ago. Go, if you like. You're your own master, I hope?"

"You keep me poor, and plunder me, and make a sport and jest of me besides," said the old man, turning from one to the other. " Ye'll drive me mad among ye."

The utter feebleness of the childish old man, contrasted with the keen and cunning looks of those in whose hands he was, smote upon the little listener's heart.

"Confound you, what do you mean?" said the gruff man. "Keep you poor! You'd keep us poor if you could, wouldn't you?" And raising his voice, "Dash me, what do you mean by such ungentlemanly language as plunder, eh?"

The old man stood helplessly between them for a little time, and then said, turning to the last speaker, "You yourself were speaking of plunder just now, you know. Don't be so violent with me. You were, were you not?"

"Not of plundering among present company," growled the gruff man.

"Don't be hard on him, Jowl," said Isaac List. "He's sorry for having given offence. There—go on with what you were saying—go on."

"*Does* he wish it?" said the other.

"Ay," groaned the old man, sitting down and rocking himself to and fro. "Go on, go on. It's vain to fight with it; I can't do it; go on."

"I go on then," said Jowl, "where I left off, when you got up so quick. If you're persuaded that it's time for luck to turn, help yourself to what seems put in your way on purpose. Borrow it I say, and, when you're able, pay it back again."

"Certainly," Isaac List struck in; "if this good lady as keeps the wax-works has money, and does keep it in a tin box when she goes to bed, and doesn't lock her door for fear of fire, it seems an easy thing."

"You see, Isaac," said the other man, "strangers are going in and out every hour of the day; nothing would be more likely than for one of these strangers to get under the good lady's bed, or lock himself in the cupboard; suspicion would be very wide, and would fall a long way from the mark, no doubt. I'd give him his revenge to the last farthing he brought, whatever the amount was."

"Ah!" cried Isaac rapturously, "the pleasures of winning! the delight of picking up the money—the bright, shining, yellow boys—and sweeping 'em into one's pocket! But you're not going, old gentleman?"

"I'll do it!" said the old man, who had risen and taken two or three hurried steps away, and now returned as hurriedly. "I'll have it, every penny!"

"Why, that's brave," cried Isaac, jumping up and slapping him on the shoulder; "and I respect you for having so much young blood left."

"He gives me my revenge, mind!" said the old man, pointing to him eagerly with his shrivelled hand; "mind—he stakes coin against coin, down to the last one in the box, be there many or few. Remember that!"

"I'm witness," returned Isaac. "I'll see fair between you. When does this match come off? Tonight?"

"I must have the money first," said the old man, "and that I 'll have tomorrow—"

"Why not tonight?" urged Jowl.

"It's late now, and I should be flushed and hurried," said the old man. "It must be softly done. No, tomorrow night."

"God be merciful!" cried Nell within herself, "and keep us in this trying hour! What shall I do to save him?"

The old man then shook hands with his tempters, and slowly withdrew.

When he was out of sight and out of hearing, they turned to each other and laughed aloud.

"So," said Jowl, "it's done at last. What'll he bring, do you think?"

"Whatever he brings, it's halved between us," returned Isaac List.

The child crept away with slow, cautious steps; then, flying homewards, she threw herself upon her bed distracted.

The first idea that flashed upon her mind was flight, instant flight; dragging him from that place, and rather dying of want upon the road, than ever exposing him again to such terrible temptations.

Then she remembered the crime was not to be committed until the next night; there was time for thinking and resolving what to do. Then she had a horrible fear that he might be committing the robbery at that moment; with a dread of hearing shrieks and cries piercing the silence of the night.

It was impossible to bear such torture! She stole to the room where the money was, opened the door and looked in. God be praised! He was not there, and Mrs Jarley was sleeping soundly.

She went back to her own room, and tried to prepare herself for bed. But who could sleep—sleep! Half undressed, and with hair in wild disorder, Nell flew to the old man's bedside, clasped him by the wrist, and roused him from his sleep.

"What's this?" he cried, starting up in bed, and fixing his eyes upon her pallid face.

"I have had a dreadful dream," said the child, with an energy that nothing but such terrors could have inspired. "A dreadful, horrible dream. I have had it once before. It is a dream of grey-haired men like you, in darkened rooms at night, robbing the sleepers of their gold! Up, up!"

The old man shook in every joint, and folded his hands like one who prays.

"Not to me," said the child, "not to me—to Heaven, to save us from such deeds! This dream is too real! I cannot sleep; I cannot stay here; I cannot leave you alone under the roof where such dreams come! Up! We must fly!"

He looked at her as if she were a spirit; and trembled more and more.

"There is no time to lose; I will not lose one minute! Up! and away with me."

"Tonight!" murmured the old man.

"Yes, tonight," replied the child. "Tomorrow night will be too late. The dream will have come again! Nothing but flight can save us! Up!"

The old man rose from his bed, his forehead bedewed with the cold sweat of fear, and, bending before the child as if she had been an angel messenger sent to lead him where she would, made ready to follow her. She took him by the hand and led him on.

As they passed the door of the room he had proposed to rob, she shuddered and looked up into his face. What a white face was that, and with what a look did he meet hers!

She took him to her own chamber and, still holding him by the hand, as if she feared to lose him for an instant, gathered together the little stock she had, and hung her basket on her arm. The old man took his wallet from her hands and strapped it on his shoulders—his staff, too, she had brought away—and then she led him forth.

Through the straight streets their trembling feet passed quickly. Up the steep hill, too, they toiled with rapid steps, and had not once looked behind. But when they reached the top, the child looked back upon the sleeping town, and on the far-off river with its winding track of light, and as she did so, clasped the hand she held less firmly, and, bursting into tears, fell upon the old man's neck; while he, subdued and abashed, seemed to crouch before her, and to shrink and cower down as if in the presence of some superior creature.

But her weakness soon was gone, and noble Nell was sensible of a new feeling within her. The whole burden of their two lives had fallen on her, she knew; and henceforth she must think and act for both.

"I have saved him," she thought. "In all dangers and distresses, I will remember that."

18

Among the Furnace Fires

At any other time the thought of having deserted the friend who had shown them so much homely kindness without a word would have filled Nell with regret and sorrow: but all such thoughts were lost in the new anxieties of their wandering life.

The night crept on apace, and morning slowly approached; and when the sun rose up, and there was warmth in its cheerful beams, they laid them down to sleep upon a bank, hard by some water.

A confused sound of voices woke her; and a man of rough appearance was standing over them, while two of his companions were looking on from a long, heavy boat, which had come close to the bank while they were sleeping. The boat had neither oar nor sail, but was towed by a couple of horses that were resting on the path.

"Hulloa!" said the man, "what's the matter here?"

"We have only been asleep, Sir," said Nell. "We have been walking all night."

"I thought somebody had been ill-using you," he said. "Where are you going?"

Nell pointed at hazard towards the west. And one of

the men in the boat called out, "You may go with us if you like."

And in another moment she and her grandfather were on board, and gliding smoothly down the canal.

The place for which they were bound was a great manufacturing town, with tall chimneys vomiting forth a black vapour. For several hours they journeyed thus till the clank of hammers beating upon iron, and the roar of busy streets, announced the end of their journey.

The boat floated into the wharf to which it belonged. The men were occupied directly. The child and her grandfather, after waiting in vain to thank them, passed through a dirty lane into a crowded street. The throng of people hurried by, intent on their own affairs; while the two poor strangers, confused by the hurry, looked mournfully on.

No one passed who seemed to notice them. Evening came on, and with it rain, and they were still wandering up and down.

"We must sleep in the open air tonight, dear," said Nell, in a weak voice.

"Why did you bring me here?" returned the old man fiercely. "We came from a quiet part. Why did you force me to leave it?"

"Because I must have that dream that I told you of no more," said Nell; "and we must live among poor people, or that dream will come again. Dear Grandfather, you are old and weak, I know; but look at me. I never will complain if you will not; but I have some suffering too."

"Ah! poor houseless, wandering, motherless child!" cried the old man, noticing for the first time her anxious face; "has all my agony of care brought her to this at last!"

"Please God," said Nelly, "we shall be in the country soon. And here," she said with pretended cheerfulness, "is a deep, old doorway—very dark, but quite dry; and warm too, for the wind doesn't blow in here—What's that?"

Uttering a half shriek, she recoiled from a black figure which came out of the dark recess. It was that of a man, begrimed with smoke, whose duty was to keep alive the furnace fire where metals were melted in a large and lofty building close by.

He asked what they were doing there, and, looking earnestly at Nell, said, "The damp streets are not the place for her." And added, "I can give you warmth; nothing else. The fire is a rough place, but you can pass the night beside it safely." And without waiting for a reply, he took Nell in his arms, and bade the old man follow.

Carrying her as tenderly as if she had been an infant, he led the way through the building, which was supported by pillars of iron, echoing to the roof with the beating of hammers and the roar of furnaces.

In this gloomy place men laboured like giants among the flame and smoke, wielding great weapons.

Through these bewildering sights and deafening sounds, the man led them to a place where one furnace burned by night and day. The man who had been watching this fire gladly withdrew, and left them with their new friend, who, spreading Nell's little cloak upon a heap of ashes, signed to her and the old man to lie down and sleep; while he, himself, took up his station on a ragged mat before the furnace door.

The warmth of their beds soon lulled the wanderers to sleep, in spite of all the deafening noises of the place.

When morning came he still was there, and sharing his scanty breakfast with the old man and the child, asked where they were going.

"To some country place," said Nell. And she inquired the way.

He showed them, then, by which road they must leave the town, and how they should pursue their journey; but before they had reached the corner of the street, the man came running after them, and, pressing her hand, left something in it—two smoke-encrusted pennies.

In all their journeyings they had never longed for the freedom of the open country as now. The noise and dirt of the manufacturing town hemmed them in on every side.

"Oh!" thought Nell, "if we live to reach the country once again; if we get clear of these dreadful places, though it is only to lie down and die; with what a grateful heart I shall thank God for so much mercy."

"It was a dreary way he told us of," said the old man. "Will you not let me go some other way than this?"

"Places lie beyond," said the child firmly, "where we may live in peace, and be tempted to do no harm. We would not turn out of it if it were a hundred times worse than our fears led us to expect; we would not, dear, would we?"

"No," replied the old man, knowing that she had saved him from crime. "No. Let us go on. I am ready. I am quite ready, Nell."

Slowly, slowly they travelled on. Her feet were sore, and there were pains in her limbs from the wet of yesterday.

Only the dreary streets! On every side, as far as eye could reach, tall chimneys, crowding on each other, frowning out their plague of smoke, obscuring the light and making foul the air!

They spent one penny in the purchase of a loaf, and lay down that night, with nothing between them and the sky;

and with no fear for herself, for she was past it now, Nell put up a prayer for the poor old man.

She lay down with a quiet smile upon her face, and slept, and dreamed of the little scholar all night long.

Morning came. She was weaker still, and yet the child made no complaint. She felt that she was very ill, dying perhaps; but she had no fear or anxiety.

They spent the other penny on another loaf, but Nell was too ill to eat. Her grandfather ate greedily, which she was glad to see.

Their way lay through the same scenes as yesterday, and towards the afternoon the old man complained bitterly of hunger. After humbly asking for relief at some few doors, and being refused, they agreed to make their way out of this last street as speedily as they could, and try if the inmates of any lonely house beyond would have pity on their exhausted state.

They were dragging themselves along through the last street of the town, and Nell felt that the time had come when she could bear no more. And now there appeared, going in the same direction as themselves, a traveller on foot, who, with a portmanteau strapped to his back, leant upon a stout stick as he walked, and read from a book which he held in his other hand.

It was not an easy matter to come up with him and beseech his aid; but presently he stopped to look more attentively at some passage in his book. Buoyed up with a ray of hope, the child shot on before her grandfather, and, going close to the stranger without rousing him by the sound of her footsteps, began in a few faint words to implore his aid.

He turned his head; the child clapped her hands together, uttered a wild shriek, and fell senseless at his feet.

19

The Schoolmaster Again

It was the poor schoolmaster. No other than the poor schoolmaster.

Scarcely less moved and surprised by the sight of Nell than she had been on recognising him, he stood for the moment without even the presence of mind to raise her from the ground.

But quickly recovering his self-possession, he threw down his stick and book, and endeavoured to restore her to herself, while her grandfather wrung his hands, and implored her to speak to him if it were only one word.

"She is quite exhausted," said the schoolmaster. "You have taxed her powers too far, friend."

"She is perishing of want," said the old man. "I never thought how weak and ill she was, till now."

The schoolmaster took the child in his arms, and, bidding the old man gather up her little basket and follow him directly, bore her away at his utmost speed.

There was a small inn within sight to which he hurried with his unconscious burden, and rushing into the kitchen, begged the people there to make way for God's sake, and laid it on a chair before the fire.

The company rose in confusion; one calling for one

remedy, another suggesting something else; but the ready landlady soon came running in with a little hot water and brandy, followed by her servant-maid, carrying vinegar, smelling salts, and hartshorn, which, being duly administered, recovered Nell so far as to enable her to thank them in a faint voice, and to hold out her hand to the poor schoolmaster.

Without suffering her to speak another word, the women carried her off to bed, bathed her cold feet, and, having covered her up warm, they despatched a messenger for the doctor.

The doctor, arriving with all speed, took his seat by the bedside of poor Nell, felt her pulse, and looked at her tongue. "I should give her" said the doctor, "a teaspoonful, every now and then, of hot brandy and water."

"Why, that's exactly what we've done, Sir!" said the delighted landlady.

"I should also," said the doctor, who had passed the foot-bath on the stairs, "I should also put her feet in hot water, and wrap them up in flannel. I should likewise," said the doctor, with increased solemnity, "give her something light for supper—the wing of a roast fowl now."

"Why, goodness gracious me, Sir, it's cooking at the kitchen fire this instant!" cried the landlady. And so, indeed, it was, for the schoolmaster had ordered it to be put down, and it was getting on so well that the doctor might have smelt it if he had tried—perhaps he did.

"You may then," said the doctor, rising gravely, "give her a glass of hot mulled port wine—if she likes wine—"

"And a toast, Sir?" suggested the landlady.

"Ay," said the doctor, in the tone of a man who makes a dignified concession, "and a toast—of bread. But be very particular to make it of bread, if you please."

Then the doctor departed, and everybody said he was a very shrewd doctor indeed, and knew perfectly well what people's constitutions were.

While her supper was preparing, Nell fell into a refreshing sleep, from which they were obliged to rouse her when it was ready. As she appeared greatly troubled at the thought of her grandfather being without her downstairs, they brought him up to eat his supper with her. And seeing that she still was anxious about him, they made him up a bed in an inner room. The key of this chamber happened to be on that side of the door which was in Nell's room; she turned it on him when the landlady had left her, for she did not know what kind of men might be in that strange place to tempt him to crime again; and she crept to bed with a thankful heart.

The schoolmaster sat for a long time smoking his pipe by the kitchen fire, thinking with a very happy face of the fortunate chance that had brought him to Nelly's help, and was anxious to hear next morning how the child was.

She was better, they said, but very weak, and would require a day's rest at the least, and careful nursing, before she could leave the house.

The schoolmaster said cheerfully that he had a day to spare—two days for the matter of that, and could very well afford to wait.

And as the patient was to sit up in the evening, it was arranged that he should visit her in her room.

Nell could not help weeping when they were left alone; and at the sight of her pale face and wasted figure, the simple schoolmaster shed a few tears himself.

"It makes me unhappy even in the midst of all this kindness," said the child, "to think that we should be a burden upon you. How can I ever thank you? If I had not met you so far from home, I must have died, and grandfather would have been left alone."

"We'll not talk of dying," said the schoolmaster: "and as for burdens, I have made my fortune since you slept at my cottage!"

Nell gave a joyful cry.

"Oh, yes," returned her friend. "I have been appointed clerk and schoolmaster to a village a long way from here—and a long way from the old one, as you may suppose—at five-and-thirty pounds a year. Five-and-thirty pounds!"

"I am very glad," said Nell, "so very, very glad."

"I am on my way there now," said the schoolmaster. "But you—where are you going, what have you been doing since you left me; what had you been doing before? Now tell me, do tell me. I know very little of the world: but I am very sincere, and I have a reason (you have not forgotten it) for loving you. I have felt, since that time, as if my love for him who died had been transferred to you who stood beside his bed."

He spoke so frankly, and so affectionately, with truth stamped upon his every word and look, that Nell felt straightway she could confide in him.

She told him all—that they had no friend—that she had fled with the old man to save him from a madhouse, that she was flying now to save him from himself, and that she sought some quiet country spot where the temptation before which he fell would never enter again.

The schoolmaster heard her with astonishment, and marvelled at the heroism of this young, frail child.

Nell's confidence in him was soon rewarded; and, talking more with her, he arranged that the wanderers should accompany him to the village whither he was bound, and that he would do his best to get them some humble occupation by which they could earn a living.

"We are sure to succeed," said the schoolmaster, heartily. "The cause is too good a one to fail."

They arranged to proceed on their journey next evening, as a stage-wagon, which travelled for some distance on the same road as they must take, would stop at the inn to change horses, and the driver, for a small sum, would give Nell a place inside.

A bargain was soon struck when the wagon came. Nell was comfortably bestowed among the soft packages, and the wagon rolled away, her grandfather and the schoolmaster walking on beside the driver, and the landlady and all the good folks of the inn screaming out their good wishes and farewells.

What a soothing, luxurious, drowsy way of travelling it was! To lie listening to the tinkling of the horses' bells, the smacking of the carter's whip, the smooth rolling of the great, broad wheels, the rattle of the harness, the cheery good-nights of passing travellers jogging past on horseback! What a delicious journey was that journey in the wagon.

Sometimes walking for a mile or two while her grandfather rode inside, and sometimes prevailing upon the schoolmaster to take her place and lie down to rest, Nell travelled on very happily until they came to a large town where the wagon stopped, and where they spent the night.

When they had passed through the town, they entered again upon the country, and began to draw near their place of destination. They spent, however, another night upon the road, because the schoolmaster suddenly got a fidgety sense of his dignity as the new clerk, and was unwilling to make his entry in dusty shoes, and disordered dress. So next morning they all started afresh and tidy, and soon came upon their future home, and stopped to admire its beauties.

"See—here's the church!" cried the delighted schoolmaster, in a low voice; "and that old building close beside it is the school-house, I'll be bound. Five-and-thirty pounds a year in this beautiful place!"

They admired everything; the brown thatched roofs of cottage, barn, and homestead peeping from among the trees; the stream that rippled by the distant watermill. It was for such a spot as this the child had wearied; and none more beautiful than this sweet reality.

"I must leave you somewhere for a few minutes," said the schoolmaster. "I have a letter to present and inquiries to make, you know. Where shall I take you? To the little inn yonder?"

"Let us wait here," rejoined Nell. "The gate is open. We will sit in the porch till you come back."

"A good place too," said the schoolmaster, leading the way to it, putting down his portmanteau, and placing it on the stone seat. "Be sure that I come back with good news, and am not gone long."

So the happy schoolmaster put on a brand-new pair of gloves which he had carried in a little parcel in his pocket all the way, and hurried off, full of ardour and excitement.

Nell watched him from the porch until the trees hid him from her view, and then stepped softly out into the churchyard.

It was a very aged place; the church had been built many hundreds of years ago, and had once had a monastery attached; and close to the churchyard were two small dwellings with old, old windows and oaken doors.

She knew not why, but these two ancient dwellings fascinated Nell.

20

Their New Home

After a long time the schoolmaster appeared at the wicket-gate of the churchyard, and hurried towards them, jingling in his hand a bundle of rusty keys. He was quite breathless with pleasure and haste when he reached the porch, and at first could only point towards the old buildings which had fascinated Nell.

"You see those two old houses?" he said at last.

Nell said she had been looking at them all the time he had been away.

"And you would have looked at them more curiously yet, if you could have guessed what I have to tell you," said he. "One of those houses is mine." And, taking her hand, the schoolmaster, with a radiant face, led her to the place.

They stopped before its low-arched door. After trying several keys in vain, the schoolmaster found one to fit the huge lock, which turned back creaking, and admitted them into the house.

The room into which they entered was a vaulted chamber once nobly ornamented by cunning architects, and still retaining its beautiful groined roof with beautiful leaves and figures carved in the stone. A wooden screen had been constructed in one part of the chamber to form a sleeping-closet; and two old rickety, carved oak seats stood in the broad fireplace. An open door leading to a small room, dim with the light that came through the leaves of ivy, completed this ancient place.

The house was not bare of furniture, which was very old and richly carved; and there was also a great store of firewood piled up for the winter.

Nell looked round with an awed and solemn feeling. "It is a very beautiful place!" she said in a low voice.

"A peaceful place to live in, don't you think so?" said her friend. Then he added gaily, "And this house is yours."

"Ours!" cried Nell.

"Ay," returned the schoolmaster, "for many a merry year to come, I hope. I shall be a close neighbour—only next door—but this house is yours."

Having now told his great surprise, the schoolmaster sat down, and, drawing Nell to his side, told her how he had learnt that that old place had been occupied by a very old woman who kept the keys of the church, opened and closed it for the services, and showed it to strangers; how she had died not many weeks ago, and nobody had yet been found to take her place.

How, learning all this from the sexton, and acting on his advice, he had taken courage to mention his fellow-travellers to the clergyman, who had kindly appointed them to the post, and would like to see Nell and her grandfather on the morrow.

"There's a small allowance of money," said the schoolmaster. "It is not much, but still enough to live upon in this quiet spot. By clubbing our funds together, we shall do bravely; no fear of that."

"Heaven bless and prosper you!" sobbed the grateful child.

"Amen, my dear," said the schoolmaster, "and all of us, as It will, and has, in leading us through sorrow and trouble to this tranquil life. But we must look at my house now. Come!"

They repaired to the other house, and found another beautiful, old, vaulted chamber, with beautiful, richly carved furniture, and another stack of firewood too.

In a short time each had its cheerful fire glowing and crackling on the hearth. Nell, busily plying her needle, mended the window curtains, and drew together the rents that time had worn in the threadbare scraps of carpet, making them whole and decent.

The schoolmaster swept the ground before the door, trimmed the long grass, and trained the ivy and creeping plants which hung neglected; and gave to the outer walls a cheery air of home.

The old man lent his aid to both, went here and there on little patient services, and was happy.

Neighbours, too, as they came from work, gave their help; or sent their children with such small presents or loans as the strangers needed most.

It was a busy day; and night came on and found them busy still. Then they took their supper together in Nell's old, beautiful room, and sat after round the fire with glad and quiet hearts. Before they separated the schoolmaster read some prayers aloud; and then, full of gratitude and happiness, they parted for the night.

When her grandfather was sleeping peacefully in his bed, Nell lingered before the dying embers, thinking of her past life as if it had been a dream; and when she went to bed she slept sweetly, and dreamed of the little scholar again.

They were up early next morning, and worked gaily in their houses until noon, and then went to visit the clergyman.

He was a simple-hearted old gentleman, who received them very kindly, and was much interested in Nell, asking her name, her age, and her birthplace.

"She is very young," said the clergyman.

"Old in adversity and trial, Sir," said the schoolmaster, who had already told him Nell's story.

"God help her! Let her rest and forget them," said the old gentleman. But an old church is a dull and gloomy place for one so young as you, my child."

"Oh, no, Sir," said Nell. "I have no such thoughts, indeed."

"I would rather see her dancing on the green at nights," said the old gentleman, laying his hand on her head, and smiling sadly, "than have her sitting in the shadow of our mouldering arches. You must look to this, and see that her heart does not grow heavy among these solemn ruins, friend."

After more kind words they withdrew, and went back to Nell's house talking of their happy fortune, when a visitor appeared. He was a little, old gentleman, who lived with the clergyman, and had been his college friend. He was known by the simple villagers as the Bachelor, and was the mediator, comforter, and friend of everybody there.

"This is our young church-keeper?" he said, after he had greeted the schoolmaster very cordially; and he kissed Nell's cheek, and looked at her just as the clergyman had smiled—sadly.

"She has been ill, Sir, very lately," said the schoolmaster.

"Yes, yes. I know she has. There have been much suffering and heartache here."

"Indeed there have, Sir."

The little, old gentleman glanced at the grandfather, and back again at the child, whose hand he took tenderly in his, and held.

"You will be happier here," he said; "we will try, at least, to make you so. You have made great improvements here already. Are they the work of your hands?"

"Yes, Sir," said Nell.

"We may make some others," said the Bachelor. "Let us see now, let us see."

Nell accompanied him into the other little rooms, and over both houses, in which he found various small comforts wanting; and which he said he would supply from some odds and ends that he had at home; and then the Bachelor disappeared, and returned in ten minutes' time laden with rugs, blankets, and other household comforts, and followed by a boy carrying a similar load. When all these things had been put in their proper places, he charged the boy to run off and bring his schoolmates to be marshalled before their new master.

The windows of the two old houses were ruddy again that night with the reflection of the cheerful fires that burned within; and the Bachelor and the clergyman, pausing to look upon them as they returned from their evening walk, spoke softly together of the beautiful child, and looked round upon the churchyard with a sigh.

21

Fading Away

Nell was up early next morning, and having discharged her household tasks, took down, from its nail by the fireside, a little bundle of keys that the Bachelor had given her on the previous day, and went out alone to visit the old church.

It was a beautiful day; the air was clear, and the dew glistened on the green mounds in the churchyard, like tears shed by Good Spirits over the dead. Some little children were playing among the tombs, and hid from each other, with laughing faces. They had a baby with them, and had laid it down asleep upon a child's grave, in a little bed of leaves.

Nell drew near and asked one of them whose grave it was. The boy answered that that was not its name; it was a garden, he said—his brother's. And he knelt down, and nestling for a moment with his cheek against the turf, bounded merrily away.

It was easy to find the key belonging to the outer door, for each was labelled on a scrap of yellow parchment. It opened with a hollow sound, and Nell found herself alone in the solemn building.

What an old, old place it was!

The child sat down, and, gazing around with a feeling of awe, tempered with a quiet delight, felt now that she was happy and at rest.

She took a Bible from the shelf and read; then, laying it down, thought of the summer days and the bright spring-time that would come—of the leaves that would flutter at the window—of the songs of birds, and growth of bud and blossom out of doors.

Nell left the chapel—very slowly—and coming to a low door, which plainly led into the tower, opened it, and climbed the winding stair in darkness. At length she gained the end of the ascent, and stood upon the turret top.

Oh! the glory of the sudden burst of light; the freshness of the fields and woods, stretching away on every side and meeting the bright sky; the children yet at their gambols down below—all, everything, so beautiful and happy! It was like passing from death to life; it was drawing nearer Heaven!

The children were gone by the time she emerged into the porch and locked the door. As she passed the schoolhouse she could hear the hum of busy voices. The schoolmaster had begun his labours only that day. The noise grew louder, and, looking back, she saw the boys come trooping out and disperse themselves with merry shouts and play.

"It's a good thing," thought Nell; "I am very glad they pass the church."

Again that day, yes, twice again, the little keeper of the keys stole back, and, sitting in her former seat, she read from the same Book, or thought her quiet thoughts.

Even when it had grown dusk, and the shadows of coming night made it more solemn still, the child remained like one rooted to the spot, and had no fear or thought of stirring.

They found her there at last, and took her home. She looked pale but very happy, until they separated for the night; and then as the poor schoolmaster stooped down to kiss her cheek, he thought he felt a tear upon his face.

The Bachelor, too, found in the old church a constant source of interest and amusement; and many a summer day, within its walls, he sat poring over old tales and legends of the place. And it was from his lips that Nell learnt her easy task. And all that he told the child she treasured in her mind.

One day, walking thoughtfully through the churchyard, Nell came unexpectedly upon the schoolmaster, who was sitting on a green grave in the sun, reading.

"Nell here?" he said cheerfully, closing the book. "It does me good to see you in the air and light. I feared you were again in the church, where you so often are."

"Feared!" echoed Nell, sitting down beside him. "Is it not a good place?"

"Yes, yes," said the schoolmaster. "But you must be gay sometimes—nay, don't shake your head and smile so very sadly."

"Not sadly, if you knew my heart," said Nell. "Do not look at me as if you thought me sorrowful. There is not a happier creature on the earth than I am now." And she took his hand and folded it tenderly between her own.

They were seated in the same place, when the grandfather approached. Then the church clock struck the hour of school, and the schoolmaster withdrew.

"A good man," said the grandfather, looking after him, "a kind man. Surely *he* will never harm us, Nell. We are safe here at last—eh? We will never go away from here?"

Nell shook her head and smiled.

"She needs rest," said the old man, patting her cheek; "too pale, too pale. She is not like what she was."

"When?" asked the child.

"Ha!" said the old man, "to be sure—when? How many weeks ago? Could I count them on my fingers? Let them rest though; they are better gone."

"Much better, dear," said Nell. "We will forget them; or, if we ever call them to mind, it shall be only as some uneasy dream that has passed away."

"Hush!" said the old man, looking over his shoulder; "no more talk of the dream, and all the miseries it brought. There are no dreams here. 'Tis a quiet place, and they keep away. Let us never think about them, lest they should pursue us again. Sunken eyes and hollow cheeks—wet, cold, and famine—and horrors before them all, that were even worse—we must forget such things if we would be tranquil here."

"Thank Heaven!" thought the child, "for this most happy change."

"I will be patient," said the old man, "humble, very thankful and obedient, if you will let me stay. But do not hide from me; do not steal away alone; let me keep beside you. Indeed, I will be very true and faithful, Nell."

"I steal away alone! See here, dear Grandfather; we'll make this place our garden—why not? It is a very good one—and tomorrow we'll begin, and work together, side by side."

"It is a brave thought!" cried her grandfather. "Mind, darling—we begin tomorrow."

Who so delighted as the old man when they next day began their labour? They plucked the long grass and nettles from the tombs, made the turf smooth, and cleared it of the leaves and weeds. They were working hard, when the child, raising her head, observed that the Bachelor was sitting on the stile close by, watching them in silence.

"A kind office," said the little gentleman, nodding to
Nell. "Have you done all that this morning?"

"It's very little, Sir," returned the child, "to what we
mean to do."

"Good work, good work," said the Bachelor. "But do
you only labour at the graves of children and young
people? "

"We shall come to the others in good time, Sir," said
Nell, turning her head aside and speaking softly.

It seemed to strike the grandfather suddenly that they
had been working at children's graves only, though he
had not noticed it before. He looked in a hurried manner
at the graves, then anxiously at the child, then pressed
her to his side, and bade her stop to rest.

He turned so often after that, and looked so uneasily at
her, that Nell asked him why he did so. But he said it was
nothing—nothing; and, laying her head upon his arm, he
patted her fair cheek with his hand, and muttered that
she grew stronger every day, and would be a woman
soon.

From that time there sprang up in the old man's mind a
solicitude about the child that never left him. From that
time, he, who had seen her toiling by his side through so
much difficulty and suffering, awoke to a sense of what
he owed her, and what those miseries had made her.
From that time he took no thought of his own comfort;
he thought only of hers.

As weeks went on, Nell, growing weaker, and very
tired, would pass whole evenings on a couch beside the
fire. At such times the schoolmaster would bring in
books and read aloud to her. The old man sat and
listened with his eyes fixed upon the child; if she smiled
or brightened with the story, he would say it was a good
one a very good story indeed.

But Nell yearned to be out of doors, and walking in her solemn garden. Strangers, too, would come to see the church, and those who came, speaking to others of the beautiful child, sent more. The old man would follow them at a little distance, listening to the voice he loved so well; and when the strangers left, and parted from Nell, he would mingle with them to catch fragments of their conversation.

They always praised the child, her sense and beauty; and he was proud to hear them. But what was that, so often added, which wrung his heart, and made him sob and weep alone in some dull corner! Some pitying words—they always pitied her, and bade *him* good day compassionately, and whispered as they passed.

The people of the village, too, grew to have a fondness for poor Nell; and they, too, spoke compassionately. None of them, old or young, thought of passing Nell without a friendly word. And many who came from three or four miles distant, brought her little presents. The very schoolboys, light-hearted and thoughtless as they were, were sorry if they missed her in the usual place upon their way to school, and would turn out of the path to ask after her at the latticed window.

The little boy, who had called his brother's grave a garden, was her little favourite and friend. It was his delight to help her, or to fancy that he did so, and they soon became close companions.

It happened that, as she was reading in the old spot by herself, this little boy came running in with his eyes full of tears, and after looking eagerly at her for a moment, clasped his tiny arms passionately about her neck.

Nell soothed him, and asked him what the matter was.

"She is not one yet," said the boy. "No, no, not yet."

Nell looked at him wonderingly, and, putting his hair

back from his face, and kissing him, asked him what he meant.

"Why, they say," replied the boy, looking up into her face, "that you will be an angel before the birds sing again. But you won't be, will you? Don't leave us, Nell; though the sky is bright, don't leave us!"

Nell drooped her head, and put her hands before her face.

"She cannot bear the thought," cried the boy. "You will not go. You know how sorry we should be. Dear Nell, tell me that you'll stay among us."

The little creature folded his hands and knelt down at her feet. "Won't you say yes, Nell?"

She only sobbed, and her head was drooped, and her face hidden still.

"After a time," said the boy, trying to draw away her hand, "the kind angels will be glad to think that you are not among them, and that you stayed here to be with us. Willy went away to join them; but if he'd known how I should miss him in our little bed at night, he never would have left me, I am sure."

Nell suffered him to move her hands and put them round his neck. There was a tearful silence; but by and by she looked upon him with a smile, and promised him, in a very gentle, quiet voice, that she would stay and be his friend, as long as God would let her.

He clapped his little hands and thanked her many times, and ran away quite happy; but often afterwards he would come and call in a timid voice outside the door to know if Nell were there; for a sudden fear seized him at such times that she had gone to live among the angels.

"And a good little friend he is too," said the old sexton once to Nell. "When his elder brother died, I remember this one took it sorely to heart."

22

Among the Angels

When Nell told the poor schoolmaster that she and her grandfather had not a friend in the world, she little knew of one who was at that moment seeking for them—one who, with a beating heart, was following in their track to share his wealth with them, even when the wanderers passed those dreadful days among the furnace fires.

It was the Younger Brother—the younger brother of the old man, who had been a sickly child, and whom the elder brother had loved so tenderly.

He left home, you may remember, when the elder brother married the beautiful girl; and travel in those foreign lands made him strong and well. He never married; but lived a lonely life. And he grew rich. In those days it was more difficult for those travelling in strange lands to send and receive letters than it is now.

Letters betwixt the brothers were few and far between; the years went by, and the brothers became old men.

Then dreams of their early life together visited the Younger Brother more and more, with strange yearnings for the affectionate companion of those early days. With the utmost speed he could exert, he settled his affairs and arrived one evening at his brother's door—to find him gone—gone with the beautiful child, none knew whither.

Inquiring here, and searching there; for he was an energetic man, and would not give up his quest; the Younger Brother at last discovered that the wanderers had been seen with two poor travelling showmen.

His energy in time discovered Codlin and Short; and later on he traced the fugitives to Mrs Jarley's, only to be disappointed again.

"I always said it," cried Mrs Jarley. "I knew she was not a common child! Alas, Sir! we have no power to help you, for all that we could do has been tried in vain."

She told him all she knew of Nell and her grandfather, from the first meeting with them, down to the time of their sudden disappearance; adding that she had made every possible effort to trace them, but without success.

He had no other clue to follow, and, sick at heart, the Younger Brother returned to London.

Now it happened that Kit—good, honest Kit, the errand-boy—had succeeded in getting a very comfortable situation as house-boy, with a kind old gentleman and lady, a Mr and Mrs Garland. Of course, the Younger Brother had found out Kit to question him about his old master, and so had become acquainted with Mr Garland; and Mr Garland had a brother, living far from London, in a beautiful country village, and that brother was none other than the Bachelor.

The Bachelor's last letter was full of an old man and a beautiful child, who had, after many wanderings, found a safe home in that village, and from his description of them, Mr Garland had come to the conclusion that these were the very wanderers for whom so much search had been made. After more inquiries, he discovered that it was indeed so; and hastened to relieve the anxiety of the heartsick Younger Brother.

But the child—the child, the Bachelor's letter said—

had been weak and ailing; nay, more; the child was fading—fading away.

The impetuous Younger Brother was for starting there and then. He would take Kit with them. Kit would identify his old master and the child. And he besought Mr Garland to accompany him as well. They would journey in a travelling carriage journey night and day; and even then it would take two days to travel to the place.

"Pray God we are not too late again!" said the Younger Brother, as they sped away.

Speeding away—halting here and there for necessary refreshment, and waiting for fresh horses—they made no other stoppages.

As it grew dusk, the wind fell, till by degrees it lulled and died away. And then it came on to snow. The flakes fell fast and thick, soon covering the ground some inches deep, and spreading abroad a solemn stillness.

Oh, the long, long hours! The distance seemed interminable. Would they never reach their journey's end? As each was thinking within himself that the driver must have lost his way, a church bell close at hand struck the hour of midnight, and the carriage stopped.

"This is the place, gentlemen," said the driver, dismounting from his seat, and knocking at the door of a little inn. "Hulloa! Past twelve o'clock is the dead of night here!"

The knocking was loud and long, but it failed to rouse the drowsy inmates. All continued as dark and silent as before.

"Let us go on," said the Younger Brother, "and leave this good fellow to wake them, if he can. I cannot rest until I know that we are not too late. Let us go on, in the name of Heaven!"

They did so, leaving the position to renew his knocking. Kit accompanied them with a little bundle, which he had hung in the carriage when they left home, and had not forgotten since—the bird in its old cage— just as Nell had left it. She would be glad to see her bird, he knew.

The old church-tower, clad in a ghostly garb of cold, pure white, rose up before them, and a few moments brought them close to it.

Turning round to look about them, they saw, among some ancient buildings at a distance, one single, solitary light. It shone from what appeared to be an old oriel window, and sparkled like a star.

"What light is that?" said the Younger Brother.

"It is surely," said Mr Garland, "in the ruin where they live. I see no other ruin hereabouts."

"They cannot," said the Younger Brother hastily, "be working at this late hour."

Kit begged that, while they rang and waited at the parsonage gate to rouse the Bachelor, they would let him make his way to where this light was shining, and try to ascertain if any people were about. They bade him go, and Kit, still carrying the bird-cage in his hand, made straight towards the spot.

He approached as softly as he could, and listened. There was no sound inside. A curtain was drawn across the lower portion of the window, and he could not see into the room.

Leaving the spot with slow and cautious steps, Kit came at length to a door. He knocked. No answer. But there was a curious noise inside—a low moaning as of one in pain. The listener's blood ran cold; but he knocked again. Still no answer. Kit laid his hand upon the latch, and put his knee against the door. It was not locked, but yielded to his pressure, and turned upon its hinges.

The dull red glow of a wood fire—for no lamp or candle burned within the room—showed him a figure seated on the hearth with its back towards him, bending over the fitful light. The form was that of an old man, and the moaning went on still.

Kit advanced a pace—another—another still. Another, and he saw the face. Yes! Changed as it was, he knew it well!

"Master!" he cried, stooping on one knee and catching at his hand. "Dear master. Speak to me!"

The old man turned slowly towards him; and muttered in a low, hollow voice, "This is another! How many of these spirits there have been tonight!"

"No spirit, Master. No one but your old servant. You know me now, I am sure? Miss Nell, where is she—where is she?"

"They all say that!" cried the old man. "They all ask the same question! A spirit!"

"Where is she?" cried Kit. "Oh, tell me but that— but that, dear Master!"

"She is asleep—yonder—in there."

"Thank God!"

"Ay, thank God," returned the old man. "I have prayed to Him many and many and many a live long night, when she has been asleep. He knows. Hark! Did she call?"

"I heard no voice."

"You did. You hear her now. Do you tell me that you don't hear *that*?"

He started up and listened again.

"Nor that?" he cried with a triumphant smile. "Can anybody know that voice so well as I! Hush! hush!"

Motioning to Kit to be silent, the old man stole away into another chamber, and returned by-and-by bearing in his hand a lamp. "She's still asleep," he whispered. "You were right. She did not call—unless she did so in her slumber. I feared the light might dazzle her eyes and wake her, so I brought it here. She is sleeping soundly; but no wonder. Angel hands have strewn the ground with snow, that the lightest footstep might be lighter yet; and the very birds are dead that they might not wake her. She used to feed them, Sir. Though never so cold and hungry, the timid things would fly from us. They never flew from her."

Kit had no power to speak. His eyes were filled with tears.

Again the old man stooped to listen, and scarcely drawing breath, listened for a long, long time. Then he opened an old chest, took out some clothes, as fondly as if they were living things, and began to smooth and brush them with his hand.

"Her little, homely dress—her favourite!" cried the old man, pressing it to his breast, and patting it with his shrivelled hand. She will miss it when she wakes. See her—these shoes—how worn they are—she kept them to remind her of our last long journey. You see where the little feet went bare upon the ground..." He pressed them to his lips, and having carefully put them back again, went on murmuring to himself; looking wistfully from time to time towards the chamber he had lately visited.

"She was not wont to be a lie-a-bed; but she was well then. We must have patience... Who is that? Shut the door. Quick! Have we not enough to do to drive away that marble cold, and keep her warm!"

The door was indeed opened, for the entrance of

Mr Garland and the Younger Brother, accompanied by two other persons. These were the schoolmaster and the Bachelor. The schoolmaster had but gone to his own cottage to replenish his exhausted lamp at the moment when Kit came up and found the old man alone. He softened at the sight of these two friends, but took no notice of the strangers.

The Younger Brother stood apart. The Bachelor drew a chair towards the old man, and sat down close beside him.

"Another night, and not in bed!" he said softly. "Why do you not take some rest?"

"Sleep has left me," returned the old man. "It is all with her."

"It would pain her very much to know that you were watching thus," said the Bachelor. "You would not give her pain?"

"I am not so sure of that, if it would only rouse her. She has slept so very long... It is a good and happy sleep—eh?"

"Indeed it is," returned the Bachelor. "Indeed, indeed it is!"

"That's well!—and the waking. . .?" faltered the old man.

"Happy, too. Happier than tongue can tell, or heart of man conceive."

They watched him as he rose and stole on tiptoe to the other chamber where the lamp had been replaced. They looked into the faces of each other, and no man's cheek was free from tears. He came back, whispering that she was still asleep, but that he thought she had moved. It was her hand, he said—a little—a very, very little—but he was pretty sure she had moved it—perhaps in seeking his. And when he had said this, he dropped into his chair again, and, clasping his hands above his head, uttered a cry never to be forgotten.

Gently unlocking his fingers, which he had twisted in his grey hair, the schoolmaster pressed them in his own, and spoke to him softly of the child, bidding him think of all the sorrows and afflictions they had shared together.

"You do well to speak softly," said the old man. "We will not wake her. I should be glad to see her eyes again and see her smile. That shall be in Heaven's good time. We will not wake her."

"Let us not talk of her in her sleep—but as she was in the old cheerful time," said the schoolmaster.

"She was always cheerful—very cheerful," cried the old man. "There was ever something mild and quiet about her, I remember, from the first; but she was of a happy nature."

"We have heard you say," said the schoolmaster, "that in this, and in all goodness, she was like her mother. You can think of and remember her?"

The old man looked at him steadfastly, but gave no answer.

"Or even one before her," said the Bachelor... "Say that you can remember, long ago, another child who loved you dearly, long forgotten, long separated from you, who now, at last, in your utmost need comes back to comfort and console you."

"To be to you what you were once to him," cried the Younger Brother, falling on his knees before him; "to repay your old affection, brother dear, by constant care, solicitude and love... Give me but one word of recognition, Brother..."

The old man looked from face to face, and his lips moved; but no sound came from them in reply.

The Younger Brother spoke tenderly of their happy

childhood, and said that they two together would go amongst their boyish haunts again.

But the old man drew back towards the inner chamber, while these words were spoken; and pointed there, as he replied, with trembling lips, "You plot among you to wean my heart from her. You never will do that—never while I have life. I have no relative or friend but her—I never had—I never will have. She is all in all to me. It is too late to part us now."

Waving them off with his hand, and calling softly to her as he went, he stole into the room. They who were left behind drew close together, and, after a few broken, whispered words, followed him.

They moved so gently that their footsteps made no noise; but there were sobs from among the group, and sounds of grief and mourning.

For she was dead. There, upon her little bed, she lay at rest. The solemn stillness was no marvel now.

She was dead. No sleep so beautiful and calm, so free from trace of pain, so fair to look upon. She seemed a creature fresh from the hand of God, and waiting for the breath of life; not one who had lived and suffered death.

Her couch was dressed with here and there some winter berries and green leaves, gathered in a spot she used to favour. "When I die, put near me something that has loved the light, and had the sky above it always." Those were her words.

She was dead. Dear, gentle, patient, noble Nell was dead. Her little bird—a poor, slight thing the pressure of a finger would have crushed—was stirring nimbly in its cage; and the strong heart of its child-mistress was mute and motionless for ever.

Where were the traces of her early cares, her sufferings, her fatigues? All gone. Sorrow was dead indeed in her, but peace and perfect happiness were born.

The old man held one languid arm in his, and had the small hand tight folded to his breast for warmth, and looked, in agony, to those who stood around, as if imploring them to help her.

"It is not," said the schoolmaster, as he gave his tears free vent, "it is not on earth that Heaven's justice ends. Think what it is compared with the world to which her young spirit has winged its early flight, and say, if one deliberate wish expressed in solemn terms above this bed could call her back to life, which of us would utter it!"

When morning came, and they could speak more calmly on the subject of their grief, they heard how her life had closed.

She had been dead two days. They were all about her at the time, knowing that the end was drawing on. She died soon after daybreak. They had read and talked to her in the earlier portion of the night, but as the hours went on she sank to sleep. Waking, she never wandered in her mind but once, and that was of the beautiful music which she said was in the air. God knows. It may have been.

Opening her eyes at last, from a very quiet sleep, she begged that they would kiss her once again. That done, she turned to the old man with a lovely smile upon her face—such, they said, as they had never seen, and never could forget—and clung with both her arms about his neck. They did not know that she was dead at first.

She would like to see poor Kit, she had often said of late. She wished there was somebody to take her love to Kit. And even then, she never thought or spoke about him but with something of the old, clear, merry laugh.

The boy who had been her little friend came there almost as soon as it was day with an offering of dried flowers which he begged them to lay upon her breast.

Up to that time the old man had not spoken once—except to her—or stirred from the bedside. But when he saw her little favourite, he was moved as they had not seen him yet, and made as though he would have him come nearer. Then, pointing to the bed, he burst into tears for the first time, and they who stood by, knowing that the sight of the boy had done him good, left them alone together.

Soothing the old man with his artless talk of Nell, the boy persuaded him to take some rest, to walk abroad, to do almost as he desired him. And when the day came on which they must remove her in her earthly shape from earthly eyes for ever, the boy led him away, that he might not know when she was taken from him.

It was Sunday—a bright, clear, wintry afternoon—and as they went through the village street, those who were walking in their path drew back to make way for them, and gave them a softened greeting. Some shook the old man kindly by the hand, some stood uncovered while he tottered by, and many cried, "God help him!" as he passed along.

And now the bell—the bell she had so often heard by night and day, and listened to with solemn pleasure almost as to a living voice—rang its remorseless toll for her, so young, so beautiful, so good.

Along the crowded path they bore her now; pure as the newly-fallen snow that covered it; whose day on earth had been so fleeting. Under that porch, where she had sat when Heaven in its mercy brought her to that peaceful spot, she passed again; and the old church received her in its quiet shade.

They carried her to one old nook, where she had many and many a time sat musing, and laid their burden softly on the pavement. The light streamed on it through the coloured window—a window where the boughs of trees were ever rustling in the summer, and where the birds sang sweetly all day long. With every breath of air that stirred among these branches in the sunshine, some trembling, changing light would fall upon her grave.

Earth to earth, ashes to ashes, dust to dust. Many a young hand dropped in its little wreath, many a stifled sob was heard. Some—and they were not a few—knelt down. All were sincere and truthful in their sorrow.

The service done, the mourners stood apart, and the villagers closed round to look into the grave before the pavement stone should be replaced.

They saw the vault covered, and the stone fixed down. Then, when the dusk of evening had come on, and not a sound disturbed the sacred stillness of the place, with tranquil and submissive hearts they turned away and left the child with God.

It was late when the old man came home. The boy had led him to his own house, under some pretence, on their way back; and where, feeling drowsy after his long walk, he had sunk into a deep sleep by the fireside. He was perfectly exhausted, and they were careful not to rouse him.

The Younger Brother, uneasy at his long absence, was watching at the door for his coming when he appeared in the pathway with his little guide. He advanced to meet them, and making the old man lean upon his arm, conducted him with slow and trembling steps towards the house.

He went to her chamber straight. Not finding what he had left there, he returned with distracted looks to the room in which they were assembled. From that, he rushed into the schoolmaster's cottage, calling her name. They followed close upon him, and when he had vainly searched it, brought him home.

Then, with the utmost pity and affection, and dwelling with many fervent words upon the happy Home to which she had been removed, they told him at last the truth; and he fell down among them like a murdered man.

Dead! He could not bear to hear the word. They dared not mention it. He lived only in the hope of finding Nell again.

The boy—her little friend—had no longer any influence with him. Sometimes he would suffer him to walk with him, or stop to kiss his cheek, or pat him on the head. At other times he would not brook him near.

One day they found that he had risen early, and— with his staff in his hand, her own straw hat, and her little basket full of such things as she had been used to carry—was gone. As they were making ready to pursue him far and wide, a frightened schoolboy came who had seen him, but a moment before, sitting in the church— upon her grave, he said.

They hastened there, and going softly to the door, saw him waiting patiently. They did not disturb him then, but kept a watch upon him all that day. When it grew dark, he rose and returned home, and went to bed, murmuring to himself, "She will come tomorrow!"

Upon the morrow he was there again from sunrise until night: and still at night he laid him down to rest and muttered, "She will come tomorrow!"

And thenceforth, every day, and all day long, he waited at her grave for her; and still they would hear him whisper in his prayers, "Oh! let her come tomorrow!"

He did not return at the usual hour one evening, and

they went to look for him. He was lying dead upon the stone.

They laid him by the side of her whom he had loved so well; and in the church where they had so often prayed and mused and lingered hand in hand, the child and the old man slept together.